GUNNER

WOLF ELITE SHIFTERS

SEDONA VENEZ

WANT FREE SEDONA VENEZ BOOKS?

Sign up for Sedona Venez's Newsletter and receive FREE BOOKS. In addition to the free stories, you will also get special pricing, exclusive previews and news of new releases.

GET A FREE SEDONA VENEZ BOOK!

Join Sedona's mailing list to be the first to know of new releases, free books, special prices and other author giveaways.

https://sedonavenez.com/free-book

❧ I ❧

GUNNER

"Did you hear that?"

My heart thumped loudly as I fought to run, to get out of the clearing where my men and I were positioned like sitting ducks, but my body refused to obey. Instead, just like I'd relived a thousand times in the nightmare, I paused, signaling the rest of my squad to stop and look around.

Run! *I wanted to shout to my men, but my mouth opened independently as I turned toward Landon, the man who was speaking, instead, "That sound like some kind of animal to you?"*

A growl echoed across the clearing, louder than the last one we'd heard, and Eli's face tightened. "Some kind of canine, I reckon," he hissed uneasily. "I think we should clear out."

Yes! I shouted in my head as I tried to make my body move. But, once again, because of the dream, I refused to budge. Frustrated, I wished I could give myself a good kick in the ass.

What was the point of reliving this shit over and over again if I couldn't even be in control of my own body?

I knew it was just a dream, but part of me yearned to try to change it. If I could just get us out of there, away from the monsters that were about to change us forever...

"I don't think that's such a great idea," Hunter interjected. "The beast will chase us if we try to run. Why not just shoot the damn thing if it makes a move for us?"

"What if there's more than one?" Jake, another of my men, argued.

Eli shrugged. "There are five of us, all loaded up with ammunition." He hefted his M16 rifle, a devil-may-care grin on his face. "No way we can't stand up to two or three overgrown wolves."

I opened my mouth to say something, but before I could, a pack of wolves surged through the trees, jaws open, eyes gleaming red in the shade of the jungle. As I jumped back, my eyes counted at least ten of the beasts. They were bigger than any wolves I'd ever seen, with wickedly sharp large teeth and hulking muscular bodies that were twice the size I thought they should be. A cold sweat broke out across my forehead. I lifted my rifle as I swung around to face the closest beast, and then I tried to fire my gun.

But just as it always did, the blasted weapon jammed, and then the beast was upon me, teeth flashing bright-white in the sunlight before sinking into my flesh and bone.

~

"FUCK!"

My hoarse cry echoed throughout the train compartment as I sat up in my bunk. A hard crack, followed by a rush of pain in my skull, told me I'd hit the underside of the top bunk with my head, and I welcomed the ache. Partially because it meant I was awake and alive, and partially because I knew it was a thousand times better than the pain from that wolf bite.

Swinging my legs over the side of the bunk, I rubbed my shoulder where the phantom pain still lingered, grateful no one was actually sleeping in the top bunk to hear my scream. But that relief was short-lived when someone knocked at my door, nearly causing me to jump out of my skin. A quick sniff had me relaxing. It was only a human male, likely one of the train employees.

Getting to my feet, I rushed over to the door and opened it. Sure enough, it was one of the train conductors, a man in a blue uniform and cap, with a bushy silver mustache.

"Sir?" he asked, concern and suspicion evident in his pale blue eyes. "I'm terribly sorry for the intrusion, but I thought I heard a noise. Is everything all right?"

"Yeah. I'm fine." I ran a hand through my hair. "It was just a bad dream."

"I see." Understanding flickered in the man's eyes as he took me in. "Well, good night, then. Apologies for the intrusion."

I watched the man go and sighed as I slid the compartment door shut. Now that I was awake, I might as well head to the dining car and get myself a cup of coffee—or maybe something stronger. I opened the door and made my way to the car, seating myself in one of the comfortable-looking high-backed leather booths. Soon, I was nursing a glass of scotch, savoring the way the burning liquid warmed my throat and stomach, while I stared out at the night racing past the window.

It was too bad that alcohol couldn't make me drunk anymore. If it could, I would have drunk myself into oblivion already. But, unfortunately, fate hadn't left me even that much peace to look forward to. Now, no narcotic or depressant could make me forget who, what, or where I was.

Now, there was only cold, stark reality to look forward to—or death. And as shitty as my life had become, I still preferred it to the fiery depths of hell I knew awaited me below.

Finishing my scotch, I ordered a cup of coffee and stared out at the cornfields we were passing through. A normal human would be able to see the stalks faintly in the moonlight, but with my enhanced sight, I could see them clear as day, could count the number of corn ears on each stalk that whizzed by. We were passing through Georgia now, still a long way off from my final destination—New York City. There, I had a new job and a new life awaiting me. One I could hopefully lose myself in, leaving behind my heartache and misery.

The door to the dining car opened, and I glanced up to see a woman with her daughter enter the compartment. The little girl, along with her mother, was dressed in a bathrobe and pajamas and rubbed tired eyes set into a small, round face that was blotchy from sleep. As I watched the mother go up to the counter and ask the bartender for a mug of milk for her daughter, the little girl's scent wafted toward me. She smelled of warm sunshine and jasmine, and my throat tightened. Julia, my fiancée, had smelled of jasmine, too. The scent was in the shampoo she'd used to wash her long, silky jet-black hair. Hair I'd loved to run my fingers through.

She's not my fiancée anymore, and I'll never run my fingers through her hair again.

The pain of Julia's rejection was still fresh, as if it had happened only yesterday, though it had been a month since I moved out. A month since I revealed to her the reason for my violent edge, my mood swings, and my need for solitude at times. All things that hadn't been there before I left to chase Carlos Araya, a well-known drug lord, through the dry jungle of Bolivia and run into the horror that changed me into the monster I am now.

Looking down at my hands, I hissed at the sight of my nails, which had elongated into claws while I was thinking, a clear response to my high stress levels. Taking a deep breath, I focused my mind as I'd been taught and willed my hands to return to normal. The claws shrank, the gray fur on my hands sank back into my skin, and soon, my hands appeared normal again, like those of a regular human.

But I wasn't a regular human.

I'm a monster.

"You all are now wolf-shifters," the tribe that had taken us in after the attack informed my men and me.

Once a simple soldier, now my soul was joined with that of a beast, and the two struggled to live together in harmony. I was getting better at learning to deal with it, but my beast was still quite headstrong. If I didn't allow it to come out every once in a while, it tended to find a way to break free of its own accord, something that was never good for me.

The pain of betrayal seized my heart as I

remembered the look of shock and terror on Julia's face when I'd shown her what I'd become. The anger and fear in her eyes as she'd kicked me out of her home, shouting that she didn't know who I was, that I wasn't the man she'd fallen in love with. She'd tossed her engagement ring at me as she flung her insults, and the emotional impact had felt like a bullet ripping through my heart rather than a simple gold band with a princess-cut diamond bouncing off my chest. I'd given her that ring nearly two years before when I left for war, promising her we would be married when I came back to her.

Instead, that promise now lay in the ashes of what I'd thought was a strong, loving, and unbreakable relationship.

As I watched the child collect her mug of hot milk, my heart ached at the way her little legs dangled off the barstool, the way a few of her black curls escaped her ponytail, and the way her long lashes fluttered closed in contentment as she sipped the soothing drink.

Julia and I could have had a daughter like that.

A child to whom I could have read bedtime stories while she sipped her hot milk.

The coffee mug exploded in my hand, and I hissed as shards of ceramic pierced my flesh, scattering everywhere. The little girl at the bar shrieked, nearly dropping her own mug, and the bartender came rushing around the counter, a rag in his hand.

"Sir, are you all right?"

Quickly, I stood up. "Yes," I answered, brushing the remnants of the broken cup from my clothing and trying not to be frustrated. "My apologies."

My grip had tightened on the mug without my realizing it, and it had finally shattered from the force applied by my inhumanly strong fingers.

Embarrassed, I quickly stepped aside so the man could clean up the mess. Then I paid him and made a quick exit before anyone could realize that the cuts on my face and hands were already knitting themselves back together.

Finally making it back to my compartment and lying on my bunk, staring out the window, I wondered if it would ever be possible to feel normal again.

But knowing my fucked-up luck...probably not.

❧ 2 ❧

GUNNER

AFTER FINALLY ARRIVING at Penn Station, I eyed the crowd with surprise. People were skittering around underground, pushing, shoving, and clawing, to get to their train.

"Welcome to New York," I muttered under my breath before turning from the sound of Jimmy's voice.

"Hey, bro! Long time no see." Jimmy spread his arms open wide, enveloping me in a brotherly embrace.

I returned it. It had been a while since I'd seen my old friend, and his warm, familiar presence brought me comfort I hadn't expected.

"It sure has." Grinning a little, I pulled back so I could survey my friend.

Jimmy had traded in his army fatigues for a pair of jeans and a button-down shirt, but his blond hair was still cut military-style, and his pale blue eyes were as sharp as ever. His fashionable clothing clashed a slight bit with the military man in them, but then again, I was a little more uncomfortable with the current fashions than most men.

"You look like you're still in fighting shape, though."

Jimmy grinned back, and then he reached down and grabbed one of my suitcases. "I like to keep in shape and box at a nearby gym a couple of times a week. Keeps me on my toes. Though the wife complains I watch too many boxing matches on TV now."

My smile faded a bit as I followed Jimmy as we weaved in and out of the Penn Station throng. I frowned when I saw a dude passed out on the floor and another passed out on a bench.

"It's normal, bro." Jimmy shook his head at the men. "Let's get out of here. I have car service waiting for us outside. Paying for parking is way too expensive in Manhattan."

We finally arrived outside to the waiting vehicle, and we hopped into the car while the driver stowed away my luggage as we slid inside.

It didn't take long before the driver was weaving in and out of New York traffic, but thoughts of Jimmy's wife, whom I had never met, dampened my spirits slightly. I knew it wasn't right for me to be envious of my friend, but it was going to be hard on me to watch the two of them together, with my own relationship loss still so fresh in my damn mind.

"So, how long have you and Emily been married?" I asked as we drove out of Manhattan and toward the Brooklyn Bridge. Just because I was a tad jealous didn't mean I was going to shy away from the topic like some kind of pussy.

The last time I'd seen Jimmy was over six years ago when he was honorably discharged from the Army so he could spend more time with his dying mother. It had been a sad moment for both of us, as we'd been friends during the entirety of our careers after meeting in basic training. We'd kept in constant email contact, but since Jimmy was from New York and I from Florida, we hadn't seen each other until now.

"About three years now," Jimmy answered with a smile. "I met her at Central Park where she and her coven were performing a ritual."

"Coven?" I fully turned in my seat to face him, shock along with a feeling of unease running through me. "As in, witches?"

Jimmy laughed. "It's not quite that sinister. Emily's a Wiccan, and she and her coven were depicting one of their springtime rituals. I can't really remember which one it was," he stated with a shrug. "I've never really been into that sort of thing, you know, even after three years of being married to someone who is. But that day, she was wearing a white dress with flowers in her hair, and in my mind, a picture flashed of me standing with her in a wedding dress before an altar while I slid a ring onto her finger. She says we were together in a past life." He chuckled, but a dreamy look was on his face. "Past lives or not, it's like she was made for me."

"That's great," I remarked after a moment, more than a touch envious now. "Sounds like love at first sight."

Jimmy laughed again. "And I know you don't believe in it, but I don't really know how else to explain it." A somber look passed over his face, and he carried on more quietly, "By the way, how are you doing? I know it must be tough—Julia leaving you for another man after all this time."

I winced and nodded. Jimmy wasn't a shifter, so when I called him up and asked him if he knew about any job opportunities in New York, I hadn't been able to tell him what had really happened.

"I'm getting over it," I replied slowly, wondering if the statement was true. "To be honest, I'd had a feeling it was coming. We didn't get along as well after I came home. I guess the truth is that both of us had just changed too much."

Jimmy nodded sympathetically.

It was hard on couples when one half had to go on tour and the other waited at home, particularly when they weren't married and didn't have any children to hold them to-gether. The distance and time were bad enough, but war had a tendency to harden a person. And often, men and women who came back from war were not the same people they'd been when they left. I wished it were only my personality that had changed. That was something I could seek therapy or medical help for. For what I had...well, as far as I knew, there was no cure.

"Well, brother, I know you'll get through this. You're one of the strongest people I know," Jimmy remarked, patting me on the shoulder. "And in the meantime, you've got a place to stay with me for as long as you'd like."

I nodded, looking out the passenger window as we crossed the Brooklyn Bridge into Brooklyn.

For the first time since I'd left Florida, I felt the stirrings of anxiety and unease in my heart. From what I'd heard, the city's cost of living was a serious problem and most residents were frustrated with the fact that renters faced the highest prices in the country.

I didn't have to come here. I could have called up one of my other squad buddies for help. At least they'd have understood.

Yeah, right. Like that was even remotely a

good idea. The idea of me crawling to any of them for help was laughable, even if they'd all been honorably discharged. I'd been their leader in battle, and a leader didn't expect his men to coddle and care for him. I was the one who'd cared for them. Not to mention, I was sure they had their own problems to deal with, having all been changed as I had been. They didn't need to deal with my issues.

No, it was far easier for me to turn to Jimmy for help than any of them, even if he couldn't understand my plight the way they would.

It was a good fifteen minutes before we pulled up in front of Jimmy's two-story brownstone in Park Slope. I was pleasantly surprised by the charming line of houses that reminded me of the bygone era. Some of the houses even had the novelty of oil lamps outside the entrance reflecting a glimpse of the time of no electricity.

"Wow. This is different," I said.

"Yeah. We lucked out," Jimmy announced as we walked up the steps, suitcases in hand. "Emily's grandmother purchased this house back in the seventies before this neighborhood was gentrified.

When she passed away, she willed the house to Emily. Believe me, we would never be able to afford a house in this neighborhood otherwise...especially not on my salary. I love living in Brooklyn, wouldn't want to live anywhere else. Plus, there are a lot of beautiful single women, looking for available men like you."

"Huh?"

"You need a woman in your life...to mellow your ass right out. But she has to be a wild one...free-spirited. The yin to your yang. Opposites attract..." Jimmy raised an eyebrow at my look of surprise. "Don't act so shocked, bro. I know you better than you know yourself sometimes. You're a good friend, Gunner, but you couldn't be more conservative if you had a stick up your ass, and this is one of the most eclectic places in America." He clapped me on the shoulder and laughed. "Personally, I think the change of scenery will be good for you. You need to loosen the fuck up."

With those words, Jimmy climbed the last few steps, and then he fished for his keys and opened the door. "Emily, I'm home!" he called as he led me into a cozy living room that looked absolutely nothing like any living room I had been in before.

Sure, there were couches, chairs, and a television set, but hanging on the walls were dream catchers with little pentagrams, as well as circular wooden decorations that appeared to be showcasing some kind of tree with branches and roots that curled and spread out in the same directions. Little handmade dolls depicting pagan goddesses were scattered across the mantel, as well as candles in holders carved into the shapes of moons or suns, and incense scented the air.

"I told her she could decorate the living room whichever way she wanted," Jimmy muttered to me out of the corner of his mouth. "Not every room in the house looks like this."

Before I could respond, a woman dressed in a flowing white dress swept into the room. A colorful scarf was tied around her pale blond hair, and pentagram-shaped earrings dangled from her lobes, a perfect match to the pendant that hung from her neck. Rings and bracelets sparkled on her hands and wrists, though not as brightly as her amethyst eyes sparkled when they landed on Jimmy.

"Jim!" The woman I knew had to be Emily planted a kiss on her husband's mouth. "I see you've managed to bring your friend back here safely. Why don't you introduce me to—"

She turned to face me, and the sparkle in her eyes died instantly when she set them on me. Shock flared in those amethyst depths before they hardened, and the hairs on my neck rose at the animosity I smelled rolling off her in waves.

"I'm Gunner," I tried to say warmly, doing my best to hide my anxiety.

I shook hands with Emily and sized her up, just as she was doing to me.

Could she know what I am? My stomach twisted with dread at the very thought.

"Jimmy's told me a lot about you."

"All good things, I hope." She smiled, but it was forced, and none of the warmth returned to her eyes.

"Of course, love." Jimmy hooked an arm around his wife's trim waist and pulled her against him, seeming to sense the tension in the room. "How could I have anything else to say when I've got nothing bad to report?"

Her face softened, and she leaned up to press a soft kiss to Jimmy's nose. The tender gesture sent a pang of longing through me, and I suddenly looked away, feeling as though I were intruding on a private moment.

"You're too sweet," she murmured. "Why don't you show Gunner up to his room? And I'll set breakfast out on the table. You two must be famished."

"You're the best, honey." Jimmy gave her a peck on the cheek. Then he hefted one of my bags and made for the stairs. "C'mon, bro. Let's get you settled in."

I followed him up the stairs, feeling Emily's hostile stare boring a hole between my shoulder blades the entire way.

3

GUNNER

I WAS SITTING on the bed in my room, a security guard training manual open on my lap, when I heard a soft knock at the door. My heart sank a little as I caught the delicate floral scent of Jimmy's wife, and my shoulders tensed involuntarily. It had only been an hour since Jimmy left me, having only taken the morning off from work to pick me up. I'd thought I'd be able to hide from Emily for at least a little while longer.

Apparently, it was no use. Jimmy's wife wanted to talk, and I couldn't very well deny her since I was living in her home.

"Come in," I called, turning the page of my manual.

The door opened, and I looked up as Emily stepped inside. Her shoulders were squared, but I could sense her unease by her momentary hesitation to enter the room as well as the shadowed look in her eyes.

"I see you're studying for your exam," she remarked quietly, closing the door behind her.

I glanced down at the book in my lap and then back up at her as I smiled uncertainly. "Yes, ma'am. I need to be prepared. Jimmy is going to take me to meet his boss tomorrow, and he says I'm expected to take the examination next week."

She nodded. "Good. The sooner you pass the exam and get started on your job, the sooner you can get your own place."

Her blunt confirmation of her intentions toward me wounded me more than I liked to admit, but I simply raised an eyebrow.

"I definitely don't intend to impose, but Jimmy didn't give me the impression he was trying to rush me out of here," I answered, not willing to be intimidated.

"He wouldn't since he doesn't know what you are, but I do." Emily's eyes locked on me like magnets as she drew closer, and after a moment's thought, she perched herself on the edge of the bed that was the farthest away from me.

Cautious. She's definitely being cautious.

Well, that was all well and good. If she knew what I was, then she had every reason to be afraid of me.

"Tell me, Mrs. McKinnley," I inquired, crossing my arms, "what exactly is it that you think you know about me?"

"I know you're a shifter of some kind," she remarked, raising her chin, her eyes hard once more. "And while I don't generally bear ill will to any of Mother Earth's creations, it has been my experience that your kind brings nothing but trouble, and I am not interested in upsetting the balance in our home."

My eyes narrowed. "Judge, jury, and executioner all in one, huh?" I barked a laugh and passed a hand over my face. "I guess I should have expected this though, after my fiancée's reaction when I told her the truth about myself."

I thought I saw a flicker of pity in her eyes, but her expression remained stony.

"You should have told her right off the bat," she quipped dispassionately. "Or simply not told her at all. It would have saved you a lot of heartache."

"There was no *right off the bat*," I spat, furious at her presumption. My inner beast rumbled in my chest, excited by the rage swirling in my heart, and I knew my eyes had changed to gold by the flicker of fear now in Emily's eyes. "I was a normal man when I asked Julia to marry me. I didn't become a shifter until I was ambushed by a pack of wolves in Bolivia while being chased through the jungle." My voice thickened as my fangs slid out involuntarily, puncturing my bottom lip.

She jumped off the bed as I bared them at her out of sheer frustration.

"Do you think I asked for this?" I barked, shaking with anger.

She was backed into a corner now, her eyes wide. "You're out of control," she accused, her voice shaking a little, though her back and shoulders remained ramrod stiff.

I leaned back against the pillows, taking in a deep breath, and as I exhaled, my fangs retreated. I also knew that, by now, my eye color had to be fading back to its normal silver-gray hue. "I am not," I assured calmly. "A display of emotion doesn't have to equal a loss of control. I'm not about to hurt you—or Jimmy, for that matter. He's my oldest friend, and I never would have come here if I'd thought I would be putting him in any damn danger." I lifted an eyebrow. "I have far more history with him than you, even if you are his wife."

Her eyes snapped with fire at that. "Don't presume to tell me that you have a closer relationship with my husband than I do," she spat. The ire faded from her eyes, replaced by weariness. "But since I do know him so well, I know you've saved his life twice, and he is incredibly loyal to you, not without reason." She sighed. "I won't mention any of this to him—not just because he wouldn't believe me anyway, but also because I don't want to put him in a position where he's forced to choose sides. But please, I would appreciate it if you made yourself scarce as soon as possible. I don't have any problem with you continuing your friendship with Jimmy, but your presence in our household is a danger I simply can't afford."

I nodded, unable to find fault with her logic, though I didn't know if I agreed with her fears. "I promise I won't stay any longer than I have to," I told her. "Really, you have nothing to fear from me. I'm not going to lose control and attack you or your husband."

"It's not you I'm worried about," she confessed, turning to the door. "It's the kind of trouble you're undoubtedly going to bring." She glanced at me over her shoulder. "You're not the only shifter in this city, and I wouldn't count on being left alone. Before long, you're going to stumble onto someone else's territory, and goddess only knows what you'll get mixed up in then."

The door closed behind her with a slam, and I stared at it for a long moment, her warning echoing loudly in my ears. I finally wrenched my gaze back to the manual in my lap and started to study again.

4

GUNNER

"Hey!" The door to my room banged against the wall as it swung open, and Jimmy came marching in, a broad grin on his face. "Get up, you miserable excuse for a soldier. It's time you and I went out for some real fun."

I groaned, setting the book I'd been reading on the nightstand so I could give him my full attention. "I'm a little afraid to know what your idea of *real fun* is," I replied, eyeing Jimmy up and down. Gone was the conservative security uniform he wore for work, replaced by a leather jacket, black T-shirt, and dark jeans over motorcycle boots. "If not for your hair and lack of tattoos or piercings, I'd think you were ready to go out to a rock concert."

"Not a concert but we are going to a club," Jimmy declared, "to celebrate you finishing your security training and also passing your exam."

I'd aced the exam nearly two weeks ago, and Jimmy had been so busy that he hadn't brought up celebrating at the time—to my relief. I should have known it would catch up to me sooner or later.

"Get dressed, bro. The night's in full swing now, so we have to get a jump on things if we don't want to miss any of the action."

"Yeah, no kidding," I drawled, checking my watch, which read ten o'clock. The last thing I'd expected at this hour was for Jimmy to spring a guys' night out on me. "For Christ's sake, man, I'm in bed."

"Yes, which is something we need to remedy if we're to have any hope of getting you fucked tonight." Impatient, Jimmy threw open my closet and rummaged through the clothing hanging in there. "Shit. Don't you have anything decent to wear?"

Chuckling, I crossed the room and

pushed Jimmy away from my garments. "What is this about, getting me fucked? Is that why we're going out tonight? And what does your wife think about this?" Frankly, the last thing on my mind was getting involved with another woman, not so soon after leaving Julia.

"All my wife knows is that I'm taking you out to celebrate, and she is happy I'm getting you out of the house." Jimmy clapped me on the back.

I didn't think for a second that Emily was happy I was getting out of the house as much as she was happy that I wouldn't be around to attract trouble, as she'd suggested.

"Aside from your job training, you never do anything except sit in your room and read or work out, and I'm sick of watching you mope around in here. You need to get out and experience life again. Now, hurry up and get dressed."

I glared at the door as it shut behind him. Then I sighed and looked at my closet again. Maybe Jimmy was right. I had been a bit of a recluse ever since arriving, but that didn't mean I was doing anything wrong. I just wanted to get my life in order first, which meant proving myself at my new job and getting my own place. And I still hadn't decided whether or not I wanted to try to let a woman into my life.

What normal woman would want to be with someone like me?

As soon as she found out I was part monster, she would run for the hills, and I would just suffer damn heartbreak all over again.

"You're not the only shifter in this city." Emily's voice echoed in my head.

What if I actually found a woman who wasn't human?

Getting involved with a shifter was exactly the kind of thing that would invite trouble. Invite it right to Jimmy and Emily's doorstep. That's what she didn't want and was part of the reason I had been keeping to myself. I was determined not to cause any trouble while under Jimmy's roof.

Maybe I shouldn't go out tonight. Why not just come up with an excuse? Tell Jimmy I'm not feeling well. Better not to risk the chance of running into trouble, especially when I'm out with him.

I sighed. I knew Jimmy wouldn't take no for an answer, and I also knew there was no point in my trying to tell him the truth. If

Jimmy didn't believe in the supernatural after being married to a Wiccan for three years, he certainly wasn't going to start now. Unless I showed him the truth, but I couldn't stand the idea that Jimmy would turn away from me too.

Resigning myself to a very long night, I picked out some clothes and hurriedly dressed before Jimmy really did come back and decide to drag my ass to the club in my boxers.

5

CELINE

"CELINE, if your dad could see you here now, he'd have a hissy fit," Tamara commented.

I swiveled my body on the barstool so that I was facing my friend instead of the bar counter. Tamara sat on the stool next to me with a half-full martini glass dangling from one hand. She wore a tight black miniskirt, artfully ripped to show glimpses of her creamy thighs, a cropped white top that bared her toned midriff, and black heeled booties. Her lips were glistening with red lip gloss, her black ringlets a wild and tangled mess, her smoky eyes lined with kohl, and the way she bobbed her head in time to the salsa music pumping through the speakers made me think she ought to be up on stage with the band playing in the background behind her.

Rolling my eyes, I picked up my own glass, which contained gin and tonic, and swirled it before taking a sip. "My dad would never even consider looking for me here, which is why I decided to come here in the first damn place." I pushed my black hair over my shoulder. I'd teased it into a tousled mess of corkscrew curls, not dissimilar to Tamara's, though her black hair only brushed her jawline, while mine cascaded down to mid-back.

Tamara looked at me dubiously. "Well, if your idea was to be a rebel, you could have at least dressed the damn part," she pointed out, studying my outfit.

I shrugged uncomfortably, knowing I was dressed more conservatively than my friend, between the blood-red blouse I wore beneath my leather jacket and the skintight black jeans and stiletto boots. The only skin I was baring was on my face, throat, and hands. I knew Dad wouldn't see it that way. The skintight ensemble left very little to the imagination and would be anything but con-servative in his eyes.

"If I'd known you were just going to criticize my outfit, I wouldn't have asked you to come out here with me tonight," I snapped.

She was ruining a perfectly good night at my favorite spot. Even though I hadn't been here in a long time, I loved this club because it edged a little closer toward bar-with-a-dance-floor territory. The whole scene felt fairly Miami-inspired with mojitos and drinks that came in real coconuts. The crowd was culturally diverse. The club had DJ nights or live bands that rolled out sets chock-full of rock, salsa, merengue, samba, rumba, reggaeton, calypso, and a smattering of old-school hip-hop.

It was Tamara's turn to roll her eyes. "Oh, don't be such a sourpuss," she replied and then drained her glass. "I'm just teasing you. I'm glad you're finally out of Carter's slimy little clutches, even if it is just for a little while." She signaled the bartender to refill our drinks. "So glad, in fact, that this one's on me." She winked.

I sighed and took my refilled drink.

"Good, because I'm definitely going to need it."

Tamara eyed me as she knocked back the second drink a lot more quickly than the first. "What's the deal with your Prince Charming anyway?" she asked. "Have you guys decided whether or not you're going to seal the deal? And, more importantly...finally have sex?"

I shuddered. "I've been stalling on both counts at every possible opportunity."

As the daughter of Damon Cooper, the owner of Cooper Enterprises, I was heir to a vast number of holdings, as well as one of the largest shipping companies in the United States. As such, Dad fully expected me to marry and produce an heir before he died, and since Carter was a wealthy banker, an investor in Cooper Enterprises, and more importantly, a wolf-shifter just like me, Dad considered him to be the only truly acceptable match for me. So, in an official ceremony in front of our pack, I had given my word to marry Carter and be his lifelong mate, despite the fact that he made my skin crawl.

But what no one else knew was that

Carter had, on more than one occasion, let me know if I didn't go through with it, he would destroy Dad's company. And, as the primary shareholder, it was a viable threat.

"Aw, c'mon." Tamara rubbed my back. "Carter might be an asshole, but at least he's total hotness wrapped up in a thousand-dollar suit. Isn't that what every woman wants?"

I sneered. "Maybe if she's a gold digger, which I'm certainly not." Sighing, I glanced toward the dance floor.

Patrons were swaying and grinding on each other to the rhythmic sound of a catchy salsa song the band onstage was throwing down.

A movement out of the corner of my eye caught my attention, and I turned my head to see two large, gorgeous men enter the club. The first was attractive with an open face and easygoing smile, and while he didn't really look like the club type, he had defi-nitely decided to play the part with his leather jacket and dark jeans. Behind him, looking very much as though he'd been dragged inside against his will, was a stockier man with dark hair. While he'd obviously made an effort to fit in by wearing a black leather jacket, red T-shirt, and jeans, it was clear that he was the furthest thing from a club patron and that this was the last place he'd have picked to go and enjoy a Friday night.

A misfit. Just like me. He belonged here as much as I did, and suddenly, I was dying to know why he was here tonight. *Is he simply humoring his friend? Or is there something more?*

"Holy shit," Tamara murmured from behind me. "That guy is a hybrid."

"What?" I turned back to look at Tamara, who was staring intently across the room. I glanced in the direction she was looking to see she was staring at the two men as well. "Which one?"

"That guy in the red T-shirt who looks like he wants to kick someone's ass."

"Huh?" I sniffed, and my eyes widened as I smelled what Tamara's more sensitive nose had already picked up. "You're right. He's not a pure-blooded shifter. He's definitely a hybrid shifter."

Now, that's new.

I'd met many different hybrid shifters before, usually jaguars with the occasional bear passing through, but never a hybrid wolf. The main difference between hybrids and pure-blooded shifters, like me, was that pure-blooded shifters were born with their full abilities, while hybrids were born human and then later turned. In addition, purebloods could change into their full beast and take advantage of all the many powers that came from the transformation. Hybrids could only transform into half-beast, half-man, and because of that, they weren't usually accepted into shifter packs.

"Uh-huh." Tamara leaned forward, her dark eyes alight as she smiled. "I think tonight's going to get a lot more interesting. Now, back off, girlie."

I felt a strange streak of possessiveness at the way Tamara was eyeing the newcomer, though I knew it was unwarranted.

"This one is mine," Tamara declared. "You're already taken, remember?"

I lifted an eyebrow. "Oh, really?" I asked, folding my arms. "I'm not mated to Carter just yet." *Nor do I want to be.*

"Well, I saw him first." She eyed me. "Though I'm tempted to let you have a crack at him since you haven't had sex in so long. I bet if you popped your gorgeous legs open, I'd see cobwebs."

I laughed. "So true." I playfully fluttered my eyelashes. "So why can't you just throw a dry-spell girl like me a bone?"

"I could...but I won't," Tamara replied with a smile.

"Seriously, Tamara, I don't want him. I already have my hands full with trying to dodge Carter's persistent attempts to get me into his bed. I don't need the drama of another man I'm not remotely interested in having sex with. So, hard pass on the hybrid. You're welcome to him."

"Damn! Your I-don't-give-a-shit-about-anything attitude is getting real tired. Why don't you just take a vow of celibacy and become a damn nun?" Tamara's eyes narrowed. "Where's the fun Celine hiding? Shit. There was a time when you wouldn't hesitate to walk right over to that guy and get his number."

The truth of her words hurt, but I shrugged them off like a fur coat.

"That woman has withered and disintegrated into dust," I snapped. "All that's left is me. A woman who's freaked out of her mind about a loveless, boring future with Carter."

Shit. My life is so fucked right now, and there is no way out of the box I've committed myself to. I wish I could just go back to the woman I was before I met Carter...but I can't.

"Celine, you could always tell Carter to go fuck himself and walk away from him," Tamara countered.

"I could, but I won't," I whispered.

Despite the fact that I desperately wanted to break off my arrangement with Carter, I couldn't, not without risking him ruining Dad.

I blinked back the tears.

Dad had been through enough shit after Mom died, and I refused to drive another stake into his damn heart. As much as I knew that he loved me dearly, I also knew that Dad's business meant everything to him. It was his lifeline after his true mate, Mom, passed away.

"Celine, you know my opinion about this. Just tell your dad the truth—that Carter's blackmailing you."

I growled with frustration. If the answer were only that simple, I would have told

Dad a long time ago. "Okay, Tamara, riddle me this. I tell my dad the truth, and then what?"

"He'll deal with Carter."

"Of course, my dad would, and he would do it by telling Carter to go fuck himself. And that would only piss Carter off, and he'd financially ruin Dad anyway." I arched a brow. "This is a no-win situation. If I don't marry Carter, he'll destroy my dad. And, if I tell my dad the truth, he'll forbid me to marry Carter, and Carter will annihilate my dad. It's a damned-if-I-do and damned-if-I-don't situation."

"Okay, you're fucked," Tamara conceded. "But can you at least stop acting like a broken horse? The shit is depressing."

"Bite me," I mumbled.

Tamara grinned. "See? That's the bestie I know and love. I need you to show me that kick-ass spirit that you let Carter steal from you. Go over to that guy in the red shirt and show him that he's missing out on the best damn woman of his entire life."

I blinked. "Oh, hell no. I'm not doing that shit."

"Just like I thought," Tamara crowed.

"You don't even remember how to flirt...con-vincingly with a man."

"What?" I sputtered.

"Chicken," Tamara taunted.

Damn the woman.

She knew I could never back away from a challenge.

"Want to settle this shit like real women?" I grinned and then raised my fist.

Tamara grinned. "Damn straight I do."

6

GUNNER

"WELL, that's got to be the weirdest thing I've ever seen," Jimmy muttered.

"What?" I asked while glancing around the club with its brick walls, wooden flooring, and elegant, gilded furniture. The colored lights that provided little illumination in the dark club made it hard to see what was going on in either the lounge area or on the dance floor.

"Those two chicks by the bar," Jimmy declared, drawing my attention to the bar, which was the only place that had any real lighting in the club. "Is it just me, or are they playing Rock-Paper-Scissors?"

I turned to see what the hell Jimmy was

talking about and spotted two women sitting beside each other at the bar who appeared to be doing just that. Both were dressed in black, though the one with short black hair and pale skin was baring much more skin than the long black-haired beauty with an umber skin tone alongside her. I watched as the woman with long hair scowled and then cursed as her scissors were crushed by her friend's rock.

"Three out of five!" I heard her say to the other woman, my sensitive hearing now able to pick up on their conversation, even across the room.

"No way. Don't be such a damn sore loser. Get your ass up and do it," the woman with the shorter hair ordered.

The umber-complexioned woman turned her head, and her eyes widened as they caught my gaze from across the room.

My breath hitched as I gazed into them. I'd never seen such vivid eyes. They were a sparkling emerald green, and they seemed to be drawing me straight to her. Before I knew it, I'd taken a few steps in her direction.

"Hey." Jimmy tapped me on the arm. "Already got your eye, has she? I thought you weren't looking for a woman tonight."

I knew Jimmy was just teasing me, but his words brought me back to my senses sharply, and I stopped. "No, I just thought..." I shook my head, not knowing how to explain the strange magnetism I'd felt when looking into her eyes. "Never mind. Let's just get some drinks."

"Now, that's the spirit!" Jimmy boomed, grinning again.

I tried to make for the other end of the bar from where the two women were sitting, but Jimmy steered me directly into their path. Disgruntled, I stormed off to find seats, not willing to let Jimmy bully me into talking to the women. I found a low leather couch in the corner and sank into it with a sigh, wondering when this night was finally going to be over. Tipping my head back, I closed my eyes against the headache caused by the pounding blare of the music blasting from the band.

Why, why couldn't I be reading a book at home?

"Hey, stranger."

My eyes flew open at the sound of a sexy, melodic voice coming from my left. Sitting up, I saw the woman with long, black hair reclining on the other end of the couch, her arms resting atop the back. One of her booted feet was drawn up to rest on the cushions, while the other remained on the floor. It was a brazen, provocative position that drew my attention to the outline of her full breasts, hidden though they were by her jacket, and the length of her legs, which I could see were long and thick but toned under her tight black jeans.

"Um, hey," I grunted. *Wow, that was real fucking smooth.*

I sat up straight, struggling to mask my confusion, and then stiffened as her scent hit me. She smelled like a complex mix of floral and fruity scents that was oddly seductive, but underneath it was something wild and feral and disturbingly similar to the scent of the hybrids that'd attacked me in the jungle. My lips curled back into a snarl before I could stop myself, my inner beast instantly perceiving her as a threat.

Her eyebrows rose at my reaction. She very slowly lowered a glass of beer to the table. "Whoa there, wolf. I'm not here to hurt you. Just bringing you the drink your friend ordered for you." Her voice was deep and raspy. She tilted her head in the direction of the bar.

I followed her gaze to see that Jimmy was now sitting at the bar, watching what looked like a Mixed Martial Arts fight playing on a TV mounted on the wall, with a group of other men who seemed to know him.

What the hell? I hadn't realized Jimmy was a regular here.

Turning back to the woman, I tried not to scowl at her. "Where did your friend go?"

"Who? Tamara?" She shrugged. "Probably off to find someone to dance with."

She slid a little closer to me, placing a slender hand on my forearm. Tingles of awareness shot up my arm, surprising me.

"So, you got a name, wolf?"

"Why the hell do you keep calling me wolf?" I asked with narrowed eyes. *And what the hell are you, lady?*

She smiled. "Well, that's what you are, isn't it? A hybrid wolf-shifter."

Her tantalizing scent teased my nostrils, and I found myself moving closer to her before I realized what I was doing.

"I have to admit, I've never met one of your kind around here."

"Is that right?" I tilted my head to the side. So, my sense of smell was right; she wasn't one of my kind.

She nodded. "Most hybrids passing through this area are jaguar or sometimes bear," she explained. "Not many hybrid wolves around these parts."

"So then, what does that make you?"

She arched a brow. "Ever heard of pure-blooded shifters? We're humans who can change into animals."

Her eyes changed color, her emerald green irises darkening to burnt amber, the whites of her eyes a dark gold color. I blinked, and her eyes returned to their normal color.

"Nice," I hissed. "Are there many of you around here?"

"A few of us," she admitted. "But I seem to be telling quite a lot to a man whose name I don't even know yet."

It was my turn to raise a brow. "I would have thought my friend had told you, seeing as how he sent you over here."

She smirked. "Oh, your friend didn't send

me over. I asked him if I could deliver your drink, and he told me to take my time."

I swallowed, painfully aware of the waves of heat rolling off her body, mingling with the sweet, heady scent that surrounded me. She was close enough for me to reach out and twine one of her long raven curls around my finger. I wondered whether her hair was as soft as it looked. Glancing over at Jimmy again, I saw my traitorous friend was looking our way, a self-satisfied smile on his face. He winked at me, clearly thinking he'd done me a huge damn favor by sending the woman my way, and then he turned back to the fight.

Thanks, asshole.

"You're not gay, are you?" the woman asked.

I chuckled, my eyebrows cocked. "No."

She shrugged. "Well, you look a little upset with your friend for pointing me in your direction, so I thought maybe you swung the other way. I didn't peg you as gay when you walked in, but then, this is New York."

My mind flicked back to when I'd first caught sight of her while she was playing

Rock-Paper-Scissors with her friend. *So, she saw me before that?*

My mouth dropped open as the realization finally hit me. "You two were playing Rock-Paper-Scissors over me?"

She bit her plump lower lip, which made her seem a whole lot more approachable. "Like I said, wolf, it's not every day you see a hybrid around these parts, so..."

"So?"

"Shit. This is really embarrassing." She sighed heavily. "So, Tamara dared me to put on my big-girl panties and come over here and talk to the big, bad wolf."

"Is that right?" I surprised her by moving closer to her, crowding her against the sofa, instinctively sensing I had a bit of an advantage for the first time since she'd sat down.

I might not have been looking for a woman tonight, but this beauty had clearly gone to a lot of trouble to meet me, and I couldn't help but be drawn to her fearless spunk. Slowly, I reached up and brushed the back of my hand across her cheek, drawing away some of her curls. They were just as silky as I'd imagined them to be. The soft tendrils slid against my skin, and I wondered how they might look spread out across my pillows.

"Well, where I come from, usually, when people want to get to know someone, they introduce themselves. What's your name, darling?"

She blinked and then swallowed hard. "Celine," she replied, the surprise in her eyes fading as her lips curved into a slow smile. "Celine Cooper. And you?"

"Gunner Norcross." I trailed my hand down the side of her neck, allowing my thumb to linger at the pulse point fluttering at the base of her throat. I caught the sharp spike in her scent and smelled her sweet arousal. My cock hardened. "And what did you come here looking for tonight, Celine?"

7

CELINE

THIS SHIT between Gunner and me was spiraling out of control.

Damn.

All I'd wanted to do was flirt a little, win the dare, and get the hell out of Dodge, leaving him in the dust, like ancient history. But here I was, staring into his eyes that were swirling silver pools of raw, unadulterated magnetism, like I was some lost damn puppy.

Shit. How in the hell did he turn the tables on me so fast?

Granted, he was fierce, powerful, and sexy. And, surprisingly, I was genuinely attracted to him. But whatever was brewing between us couldn't—no, shouldn't—go any further. I was going to marry Carter.

I shuddered at the thought of belonging to Carter like some object...because that was what he thought I was. Some bright, shiny trophy that he was salivating to claim and put on display on his mantel. And, if Carter found out that I had been flirting with another man, he would kill me—not that I would go down without a hell of a fight. But, nonetheless, I was to be his mate.

I was startled by my inner wolf's snide remark. *Mate? Don't you mean, his property? Carter is not the wolf we want. Now, this one... Gunner is the wolf we need.*

There's no we. You want him, I hissed back. *And, in case you forgot, I make the decisions around here.*

My inner wolf snorted before saying, *Then make the decision to live a little. If we can't have this one as our mate, at least let's have a little fun with him tonight.*

I hated when my inner beast was right.

What would be the harm in enjoying my time with Gunner?

I could shed all my inhibitions for one night, letting my sensual side come out to play. And, when the night was over, I would slink back to my vanilla life with nothing to look forward to but the dread of a loveless relationship with a man I was marrying for the sake of my dad.

With my mind made up, I purred, "I think I should be asking *you* that question." Placing a hand on his chest, I continued, "What did you come here looking for tonight, Gunner?" The gesture was meant to put a bit of distance between us and give me some space to plan my next move, but electricity raced through my arm at the contact, and I fought the sudden accompanying urge to pull him closer instead. "New York might be a big place, but it doesn't take much for me to be able to tell you're not from around here."

"I'm not."

Gunner's eyes flickered, cooling a little, and I immediately regretted changing the subject. I wanted him looking at me with that hot, molten gaze, as if he were a starving wolf and I was a delicious steak that had been served up to him on a silver platter.

"Just here for a few days, visiting a

friend." He jerked his head in the direction of his friend at the bar. "My home is Florida."

"I see."

His scent changed, telling me that he was lying, but I wasn't sure which part of what he'd just said he was lying about. Deciding none of it was important right now, I filed that tidbit away to reexamine later.

"Well, how do you like New York City?" I asked, tilting my head up so that my mouth hovered just beneath his chin.

He had a strong, well-defined chin, perfect for me to lick and nip if I wanted to. I resisted the temptation but only *just*.

"It's absolutely nothing like back home," he answered, a note of real honesty in his voice. Something dark flickered in his eyes that spoke of sadness and pain, but he quickly masked it. "I haven't decided whether or not I like it here yet."

"Well, I hope you're here long enough to give it a chance," I murmured. "There's a lot to see and enjoy in New York."

I suddenly wished I could be the one to show him around to all the boroughs. To walk around Manhattan or Brooklyn, and enjoy all the sights, sounds, restaurants, and shops. Despite being overcrowded, the city was beautiful. I knew that because I had spent nearly my whole life here.

But, of course, I couldn't be his chirpy tourist guide. I had Carter and the reality of my fucked-up life to get back to. Besides, Gunner was just visiting and would be gone in a few days.

But I refused to think about tomorrow. I would just focus on the here and now...with Gunner.

"Let's dance," I coaxed, grabbing his hands with both of mine and pulling him to his feet with a seductive smile.

I wiggled my hips to the beat, tugging him toward the dance floor, but he resisted.

"I'm not much of a dancer!" he shouted over the music.

"Come on. Live a little," I countered as he finally allowed me to drag him onto the dance floor. I swayed, enjoying the exuberant energy of the salsa rhythm.

Gunner leaned in, and his lips brushed against my ear. "I don't know what I'm doing."

I grabbed his hands, placing them on my hips, and moved my body to the beat, loving the pressure of his hands on my hips a little too much.

The beat of the music thumped as he looked at me with a question in his eyes while his hands squeezed my hips. "You know how to dance to salsa?" he asked.

"Of course. Let me show you."

I pressed my hips against his sensually as I took my arms and placed them over his shoulders. His hands released me to slide along my back. Sighing, I allowed my body to caress his muscular frame, my hips gyrating to the beat, and my body stirred.

At first, he didn't do anything, but the constant bumping and jostling from other dancers forced him into an awkward yet somehow adorable rhythm.

"I don't know how you got me into this!" Gunner shouted over the music. "I swear, I've never gone dancing in my damn life."

"But you're a natural!" I shouted back as he spun me out and then in again.

He pulled me flush against him, so my breasts were mashed up against the bottom of his rib cage. He was quite a bit taller than me. When I looked up, my breath caught at the sparkle in his silvery eyes and the grin that transformed him from brooding to utterly charming. Now, we were close enough to kiss, and I knew if I just tilted my head up a little more—

"Ow!" I yelped after someone smacked into Gunner's back, causing his forehead to collide with mine, driving away my lust-fueled thoughts and replacing them with a throbbing ache. "Fuck. That shit hurt." I scowled at the person over Gunner's shoulder who seemed completely oblivious to the fact that he'd ruined my almost-there kiss.

Gunner smiled, a knowing look in his eye. "What do you say I buy you a drink?" he asked. "Since you were nice enough to bring me mine earlier."

"Well, that sounds like the best idea I've heard all night."

We ended up on one of the love seats in the corner of the lounge area, draped in shadows and slightly more tucked away from the noise than the other seating areas. Gunner got a whiskey sour for himself and a White Russian for me. I sat next to him now, appreciating his body heat and the drink.

"So, what do you do for a living?" he

asked, hooking an arm around my shoulder and drawing me into his hard, muscular body.

He'd taken off his leather jacket, and I saw the ridges of his muscles through the thin cotton of his red shirt. Though shifter men were naturally muscular and in good shape, until now, I hadn't known if the same applied to hybrids. But I had the feeling Gunner had probably been this way before he was changed.

"Who? Me?" I blinked, slightly flustered by the question. I didn't exactly want to tell him I was the daughter of a billionaire and didn't need a job. "Oh, I sell stocks and bonds and such," I confessed, going for a half-truth instead.

"You're a stockbroker?" he asked, his eyes widening in disbelief. "Damn, I never would have thought it by looking at you."

I shook my head. "I don't sell for other people. Just myself. I have a knack for investing." Dad had taught me well, and I reveled in the game of predicting the stock market, even if I only dabbled in it. "What about you?" I asked, wanting to shine the spotlight away from me.

His eyes darkened a little, but he didn't

look away. "I'm retired from the armed forces," he remarked. "Was in Special Ops when I was honorably discharged. I was in the military for five years, so I haven't quite figured out what's next for me yet."

"Mmm, so that's where you got these killer abs from," I teased, running my hand up his abdomen.

The tension eased from his face, and his eyes lit with desire, chasing the shadows away. He tilted his head down toward mine again, so our lips were only centimeters apart. My breathing quickened.

"You've got a milk mustache," he murmured, reaching up with his thumb to rub away some of the moisture that had clung to the skin above my upper lip.

Before I could say anything, he leaned in and licked the rest of it off with a slow, languid glide of his tongue against my skin. It should have been weird, but the motion was strangely sexy, and the sensation sent a shiver of desire through me.

Fuck it.

I ran my tongue against his lips just to test the chemistry, but when he tugged on my lower lip and kissed me hard, we went from playful flirting to full-throttle fuck mode. Before I knew it, I was pressing my lips against his, and then his arms were around me while he kissed me back. His lips were smooth and firm against mine while the barest hint of stubble brushed my chin. Heat erupted everywhere my body touched his, and I gasped, allowing his tongue to slide into my mouth.

I loved the way his fingers slipped into my hair, gripping it by the handful, as he held me still so he could plunder my mouth with his tongue. I enjoyed the sparks of heat flying in the air around us. Took pleasure in the way my heart was galloping in my chest. The way my cunt throbbed with the need to have him deep.

A growl rumbled in his throat. Greedily, I inhaled the masculine scent of his arousal that lingered deliciously around us. It had been so long since I actually craved the touch of a man that I was delirious from the lust breaking through the dam I'd built inside myself the day Carter walked into my life. A dam I'd thought would make him lose interest in me as a sexual conquest...but it did not. I buried all my wants and needs behind that barricade to protect myself from that monster of a man. Now, all the lust and want that I'd thought had withered away and died months ago was unleashed by Gunner with just one touch.

"Let's get out of here," he murmured against my skin, pressing openmouthed kisses that ended in delightful little nips along my jawline and down the column of my throat.

I froze. *Do I really want to have sex with Gunner?*

My inner beast screamed, *Hell yes!*

And, just like that, I made the decision to throw caution to the wind and do what I wanted—no, *needed* for once in my life.

Somehow, I'd managed to get into a position where I was loosely straddling him, and a bolt of excitement shot through me as I felt his erection—thick, big, and hard—pressing against my inner thigh. Lust whipped through me like a tornado. It wasn't long before my fingers were stroking his hair as his fingers walked down my back and landed on my backside before squeezing my ass.

I tilted my head back, looking at him. "Yeah, let's," I murmured.

"Any place in particular you think we should go?" he inquired, pulling away from my skin.

I whimpered at the loss of contact and angled my head forward to look at him. His eyes were molten pools of silver, and I felt as if they could scorch my very soul if I let him.

"Hmm..." I thought for a moment, something in the tone of his voice telling me he wasn't quite willing to take me back to his place. Normally, that would be a bit strange, but if he was here from out of town, staying at a friend's house, I could understand not wanting to offend his host or hostess by bringing home a strange woman. And I honestly wasn't interested in bringing him back to my place, not for a one-night stand. "There's this hotel a few blocks down."

"Sounds good to me," he grunted.

WE LEFT THE CLUB, HEADING NORTH through Manhattan. We'd checked the club for our friends, but neither Jimmy nor

Tamara had been anywhere in the building. I sent a quick text to Tamara, letting her know I was leaving with Gunner and where I would be, but I was surprised when he wasn't worried in the least about Jimmy.

"He probably took one look at us on the dance floor and decided his work for the night was done," he stated with an unconcerned shrug when I'd asked.

I stuck my hands into my pockets, shivering a little from the cold. It was November, and biting winds were blowing through the streets.

"You cold?" Gunner asked, looking down at me with concern. Before I could answer, he reached out and tucked me into his side protectively, surrounding me with his delicious body heat.

"Thank you," I murmured as the warmth flooded me.

I couldn't help but smile as I remembered the way he'd opened the door for me when we left the club and the way he'd smoothly but firmly ushered me to the side of the pavement, away from the street. There was something of a gentleman inside him—or at least, a man whose mother had raised him to treat women properly.

After another block, I directed him to turn on a quiet cobbled back street in the middle of SoHo. "Here we are," I announced, pointing at a small building with a sign on the front that said, *SoHo Garden Inn.*

"Here?" He blinked at the ultra-modern glass façade.

"What? Were you expecting a Motel 6?" I teased.

"Well, maybe."

He shuffled a little uncomfortably, and I realized he was thinking about the price tag.

"It's owned by a friend of mine," I hurried to reassure him.

It was another half-truth. The inn was actually owned by Dad. It was one of the more whimsical purchases Mom had talked him into buying before she died, and all because she'd simply fallen in love with the quaint charm of the neighborhood.

"So, I never have to pay here."

He raised an eyebrow. "Do you come here often?"

"If you're asking if I make a habit of

picking up strange men in clubs…the answer is hell no. You are the first one, hybrid, but don't let that shit go to your head." He opened the door for me, and I sashayed into the discreet and elegant lobby without another word.

"Damn, you're so feisty," he muttered before chuckling and following quickly.

Soon enough, we were checked into a room on the ninth floor, offering stunning views of the rooftops of SoHo.

"Shit. Isn't this classy?" He sat down on the white bedspread, kicking off his boots, as he looked around the room.

We'd gotten a suite with a beautiful scheme of gray, orange, and almond, colors. There was a large living area but we'd moved into the adjacent oversized bedroom with a deep bed. The elegant curtains were pulled back to reveal the floor-to-ceiling warehouse style windows overlooking the Big Apple. I would have preferred a more modest room versus this over-the-top luxury because I didn't want to freak him out too much. But unfortunately, this was the only room available tonight. Gunner had a dominant personality; I knew he would be highly uncomfortable if he found out I was rich and that the night was on my dime—even if that really meant Dad's dime. Something told me that Gunner was the kind of man who prided himself on being a good provider.

I stared at him. *Handsome. Respectful. Responsible. And, damn...he's sinfully sexy. Why on earth isn't he settled down with a mate or a human wife?*

He was what every woman wanted—at least, if you didn't consider the hybrid wolf-shifter part. But even then, there were still plenty of hybrids that wouldn't mind settling down with a man like him. Supernatural or not, women really weren't very different from species to species. They all wanted a man who was strong, sexy, and able to provide for them.

"Celine? Why are you looking at me like that?"

I blinked. "Like what?"

"Like you're trying to pull out all my secrets through my eyes." He stood up and then shrugged out of his jacket. He placed it on the small wooden table that sat between two wingbacked chairs by the windows.

"Maybe I am," I suggested, moving closer. I slid my hands up his shirt, and I let some of my inner wolf shine through my eyes as I grinned at him, feeling the silky-smooth skin over his muscles. A light dusting of hair teased my palms, and I began pulling off his shirt the rest of the way, so I could see all of him. "My mind tends to wander when I'm not doing anything. Maybe you could find a way to keep it...occupied."

He clasped my wrists in his hands before I could pull his shirt off all the way, and we hovered just at the top of his rib cage. Swallowing, I looked down to see the hard buds of his nipples jutting through his T-shirt, and I was struck by the urge to lean down and bite one of them.

"Are you sure you want to do this?" he whispered, his silver eyes soft.

I looked up at him, and my heart melted a little as I realized he was asking me for permission. Something the average man definitely wouldn't have done after all the signals I'd put out up to this point.

"I'm sure," I murmured, leaning in so that my lips were barely brushing his. Then, I deliberately chose my next words to push him over the edge. "So, if you don't start touching me now, I'll have to do it myself."

$$\text{❦}\quad 8 \quad\text{❦}$$

GUNNER

THE CHALLENGE in Celine's words snapped what little control I had left. I pushed her up against the wall, claiming her mouth with barely restrained ferocity. The little vixen had riled me up to a fever pitch with her seductive smiles, glances, touches, and then that fierce, hot kiss she'd given me back at the club. Her fire drew me in like a moth to a flame, and while I knew it would be all too easy to get burned, I couldn't stay away.

After all, this is only going to be a one-night stand, right?

Thoughts of Julia briefly flickered in my mind—her dark hair, eyes, and gentle loveliness that were so completely different from

Celine's sexy, wild, and unrestrained beauty. Suddenly, Celine dug her fingernails into my ass, and those images were burned to ash as lust consumed all available space in my mind. Groaning, I lifted her so she could hook her arms and legs around me. Then I staggered over to the bed and deposited both of us onto it.

"You're gorgeous," I rasped, pulling back so I could stare down at her.

Her hair was spread along the crisp white sheets, and it was just as brilliant as I'd thought it would be. Her dark umber skin was flushed with desire, and her plump lips were swollen from my ravaging kisses. And I wasn't kidding about her beauty. She had exquisite, almost pixie-like features. The tip of her nose was slightly uptilted, her cheekbones high and prominent, and her chin was not quite pointed, as it completed the heart shape of her face.

"I want to see the rest of you."

"Yes," she whispered huskily, reaching up to unzip her leather jacket.

I gently brushed her hand away, wanting to do it myself. Slowly, I unzipped the jacket, revealing the red blouse beneath it that was a stark contrast to her hair and cut low enough to reveal the tops of her breasts. Desperately wanting to see them, I pulled her tank top down and scooped one globe out of the black bra beneath. It was round and firm, nicely filling my palm, the chocolate-hued nipple hardening into a perfect bud. My mouth watering, I leaned down to taste, flicking my tongue up and down the bud.

"Oh, damn."

Her answering moan sent a thrill through me, and my lips curled as she moved her legs to clamp around my hips, dragging me closer to her.

"Don't stop," she begged as I drew her nipple fully into my mouth and began sucking. She stared at me through heavy-lidded eyes, her gaze lust-filled.

Damn. She had the sexiest eyes I'd ever seen.

I gently kneaded her other breast, switching back and forth between them until she was squirming and clawing at my jeans, trying to get them off.

"My little wolf is impatient, I see," I teased with a chuckle, pulling back. Deciding I liked the way her breasts hung out of the tank top, I left them there and popped the top button on her jeans instead. "Don't worry. I'll take care of you."

"Gunner, I want your clothes off," she demanded.

She tried to sit up, but my hands slid to her jaw before my lips settled across her mouth. Her breath caught. My tongue slid between her teeth. My kiss was long, slow, and deep—the stamp of my utter possession. When she softened in my grasp, I gently eased her back onto the bed and slid her boots, jeans, and panties off.

She gasped as I hooked her legs over my shoulders. Settling myself between the V of her thighs, I went after her pussy voraciously. My tongue lapped from her clit to the end of her cleft before swirling around her clit. I flicked it and then sank my tongue inside her. She panted with her hips arching. Holding her still, I fucked her unrelentingly with my tongue. She hissed as I worked her into a frenzy, using long, sensual licks. My tongue constantly teased her opening. My name was a passionate plea on her lips, spurring me on, and I wanted to feel her come in my mouth.

Showing her no damn mercy, my tongue

flicked her swollen nub until she screamed, "Oh my fucking God!" and bucked as I continued to lave her with my mouth.

Thrusting two fingers into her trembling channel, I curved them inside her while pressing my thumb on her clit so my hand was clamped around her. I shoved another finger inside her, making her cry out and buck.

"Oh God, yes," she moaned, her fingers digging into my scalp as she shamelessly rubbed her pussy against my face. "Yes, yes, yes!" she screamed as she came, her juices flowing freely.

I greedily lapped it all up, feeling an immense satisfaction at having pleased her. I'd never made love with a woman who burned quite as hot as she did, and strangely, something about her made my inner beast growl. For once, the two souls within my body were in complete damn harmony.

Finally, her cries quieted into a sigh of contentment as she relaxed back down onto the bed. "Wow," she breathed, eyes closed. "That was really good. I think I'm ready to turn in now." Her lips curled up into a smile.

"Hell no, you aren't," I growled, pulling

out a condom from my wallet before strip-ping off the rest of my clothes.

I tore the package open with my teeth and quickly took out the latex. In seconds, I sheathed my cock. Her eyes flew open as I pulled her up into a sitting position and re-moved her tank top.

"You're going to come at least a few more times before I'm done with you, darling."

"Well, that sounds really promising."

Her lips curved into a seductive smile that I quickly wiped off her face when I lifted her onto my lap and impaled her with my stiff shaft.

"Holy shit!" she groaned, sucking in a breath. Her eyes closed before she moaned in pleasure.

I couldn't help my own moan at the feel of her tight slit squeezing my rock-hard cock. Her inner walls pulsed around me, hot and wet, and it was so exquisitely good that I al-most came right there. But I wasn't some horny teenager who couldn't control himself. I took a deep breath through my nostrils to calm myself before gripping her hips and starting to move her against me.

"Celine, open your eyes," I demanded. "Look at me while you're riding me."

Her eyes fluttered open, blazing gold, and I could see my own irises glowing gold in their reflection. She slid herself up on my shaft and then back down, slowly working my cock in and out of her. Hissing, I squeezed the globes of her curvy ass, and then I took one of her nipples into my mouth. Her breasts hovering close by was too great a temptation to resist. I was rewarded with her growing mewls of pleasure, and I began pumping my hips up to meet hers, forcing her to increase her speed, until I could hear the sound of her flesh slapping against mine, our sweat-slicked skin gliding against one another.

Her inner walls clenched around me, and she cried out, "Gunner," before she broke apart, shuddering all around me.

I growled before sitting up, gripping her hips, and rolling her onto her back. I started thrusting into her harder as I got closer to my own peak. Her eyes rolled to the back of her head with another orgasm just as I felt the wave of my climax approach. My entire field of vision went white, hitting me with the force of an oncoming train. Colors exploded in front of my eyes, swirling kaleidoscopes, seeming to coalesce into two separate figures dragged together like magnets and then merging as one, drawing all the colors into one big sphere that eventually burst into shimmering light.

I might have tried to dissect what the hell I'd just seen if my mind weren't so completely overtaken by the sheer, unadulterated pleasure of being inside Celine and fucking her hard. My body convulsed, and I collapsed, breathing hard into her neck.

Holy shit! What the fuck just happened?

9

CELINE

"DAMN," Gunner muttered into my ear, his weight pressing me into the mattress, his heart galloping against my chest. "That was the best orgasm I've had in...shit...since I don't know when."

I knew I should answer him, but I couldn't. I was trying to avoid a damn panic attack, something that was becoming increasingly difficult with Gunner on top of me. "Can't...breathe..." I managed to choke.

"Oh. Damn. I'm sorry." Gunner immediately rolled off me, concern in his eyes, which had faded to silver gray once more. When we had been having sex, his irises had been a fiery gold. "Did I hurt you?" He reached out to stroke my cheek, a tender gesture that made my heart ache. "I thought you were enjoying it."

"I was," I quickly shot back. "I did. I am." Realizing I was babbling, I grasped his fingers, pressing them to my lips to stop myself from talking. It was the truth. I had enjoyed myself immensely, more than I had with any other lover I'd ever had. At first, I'd simply chalked it up to his raw sexual prowess, but that was before our simultaneous orgasm when the swirling colors had danced before my eyes, bringing a message from the gods and goddesses that every shifter waited to receive, some even going their entire lives without ever getting it.

Gunner is my true mate, and I can't have him.

"Good," he replied, sounding relieved. He pulled me in close, snuggling against my chest. "I was worried there for a moment at the end. It's been a while for me," he admitted. "I thought maybe I'd lost it."

"You haven't lost a damn thing," I assured him, trying to sound relaxed and satisfied, like I should be, instead of strung tight as a bow.

This certainly wasn't his fault, any more

than it was mine. From his reaction, I gathered he had no idea what the vision we'd just shared meant—or that it even was a vision.

It hurt like a motherfucker that the one thing I wanted—him—wasn't remotely possible. Not now...not ever.

Damn. Why do I have such fucked-up luck?

Blinking back tears, I took a breath and tried to distract myself with what he'd said to me. "I wouldn't have guessed it had been a while for you," I mused, running a hand down the side of his rib cage where his skin was smooth and taut.

He stiffened a little, but I could tell by the way his pulse was slowing he was on his way to la-la land. "Had a fiancée," he muttered sleepily, burying his face into my hair. "She left me. She wanted more...human."

I felt a pang in my heart at his words. There was a serious heartbreak and pain lying beneath them. It was a story I knew was all too familiar among those who had been changed. Once turned, they often lost their friends, family, or loved ones—many times, all of them. It was hard to try to coexist closely with humans when half of you wasn't one. I was glad I'd been born into a shifter family. At least I'd been raised with people who understood me. I had been taught from an early age how to blend in among the human population. I couldn't imagine how hard it must have been for Gunner.

A thought popped into my head about that, but looking up, I saw he was fast asleep. I stayed where I was, tucked into his arms, for a few moments, and then I gingerly eased myself out and gently tucked a blanket around him. He stirred once, mumbling something, and I couldn't help but smile at how peaceful he looked in sleep, almost childlike. Certainly nothing like the forbidding hybrid shifter and ex-soldier I knew he was.

We could stay with him, my inner wolf suggested. *No one would blame us, and after all, he is our true mate.*

Her words were so tempting...but, no, I couldn't do that to Dad. Though my relationship with my dad had grown distant and strained as of late, he was still the only family I had left, and I loved him dearly. And, as much as I hated Carter, if Dad needed me to marry the bastard, then I would do it...for him.

I began pulling on my clothes and boots. Marrying Carter was the only way to make sure Dad's company stayed intact. I realized there was no point in holding out anymore, not when the gods and goddesses had shown me my true mate was someone Dad would never in a million years agree to let me marry.

Finished dressing, I stood over Gunner, taking one last long look at him. *He is nothing like Carter.* That was probably why I had been drawn to Gunner in the first place.

Pushing down my emotions and swallowing the lump in my throat, I turned and left before I could change my mind and crawl back into bed with him. I knew, if I did, it would be for forever.

10

GUNNER

I AWOKE, cracking my eyelids, and stared into an unfamiliar room. I quickly sat up, trying to figure out where the hell I was. Gray walls and floor-to-ceiling windows stared back at me, and I swung my legs over the bed to get up. Then I realized I was stark naked rather than in my usual boxers.

What the hell?

The smell of wild roses, sunshine, and sex hit my nostrils, jolting my brain fully awake. Twisting around to look back at the bed, I half expected to find a naked woman with wild raven curls sprawled across the white cotton, and I felt a pang of disappointment when I saw only rumpled sheets.

Celine, I remembered.

I detected an ache in my heart that surprised and bewildered me. I hadn't known her very long, and it had been clear that this was only meant to be a one-night stand.

So, why the fuck do I miss her?

Leaning over, I sniffed the sheets, which were still laden with her scent. I growled, recalling the feel of her satiny skin beneath my lips, the sensation of her locks wrapping around my fingers, her sweet, melodic voice crying out my name over and over in ecstasy.

Damn...what a night...

A flash of black lace caught my eye, peeking out from between the sheets. Tugging on it, I pulled out a pair of black lace panties, and my breath caught in my throat. Somehow, this scrap of fabric was the confirmation that the woman I'd had mind-blowing sex with last night truly existed.

Shit! And, now, she's gone.

I felt another pang, this one sharper than before, and I clenched my hand around the fabric, suddenly angry with myself.

Why the hell am I acting like some damn jilted lover?

We'd had what we'd had, and she'd gone

back to her normal life, just as I should be going back to mine. Not that I had anywhere to be since today was Saturday. Still, I had laundry to wash and fold and shirts to iron, and a book was sitting on my nightstand, waiting for me to finish it.

Damn, is this what I've been reduced to? Security guard by day and a lonely man by night?

When had I started to be afraid to live my life?

Since I no longer knew what my life was supposed to be about.

But the longing in my heart did not fade, and I knew, for whatever reason, it wouldn't until I found Celine again. Somehow, she'd wormed her way into my head, and I was going to have to find her so I could pry her ass out of it.

Only problem was...

Where the hell am I going to look?

~

"WELL, YOU'RE BACK LATE," JIMMY remarked as I shut the door behind me. "For a while there, I was worried you were never going to come home."

"Yeah, same here." I wiped my dirty, rain-slicked boots and pushed my wet hair out of my eyes.

I'd sent him a quick text earlier this morning to let him know I was going to be running errands and would be home early afternoon, but that had turned into early evening as I scoured the city for any signs I could find of Celine. A downpour had caught me at sunset, forcing me to finally make my way back to Jimmy's.

"For a while out there, I thought I was going to get swept straight out into the Hudson River."

"It would have served you right if you had been," Emily declared briskly, bustling into the living room with a towel and a blanket.

She handed the first to me, and I gratefully accepted it, patting myself dry.

"I have no idea what was going through your head, walking about in the rain like that. You could have caught pneumonia."

"Obviously, I wasn't thinking very much," I answered with a rueful smile intended to disarm her.

There was no point in telling her I couldn't catch pneumonia—or any of the usual human diseases for that matter. At least not according to Guadalupe, the wolf-shifter chieftain of the Achamuco tribe who had taken in my squad, teaching us everything they knew about how to survive as shifters.

"I apologize."

Slightly mollified, Emily nodded. "Sit down and let me bring you some coffee, so you can warm up."

"What kept you so long, bro?" Jimmy asked, putting down his newspaper. "Must have been important. You didn't even stop by the house for a change of clothes." He raised an eyebrow.

I shrugged. "I just decided I wanted to do some exploring. I was struck by the need to get my feet moving." The latter was true, and while I had gotten to see a fair amount of the city, I'd only been looking for one thing, and I hadn't found her.

"Oh, yeah?" Jimmy smiled. "Well, I'm glad you finally decided to get out of the house." He waited until Emily had brought me a mug of coffee, and when she left, he added in a lower tone, "I guess hopping in the sack with a new lady must have been good for you, after all!" He waggled his eyebrows.

I would have laughed if not for the fact

that I was still highly confused about what the hell had happened between Celine and me last night. I settled for a faint smile instead. "I guess you're right. She sure was something else."

"Yeah, no kidding." Jimmy carefully studied me. "You planning on seeing her again?"

"Don't know," I retorted with a shrug, trying to act nonchalant. "She was gone when I woke up this morning. So, unless we run into each other, it's doubtful." I sipped the coffee Emily had brewed for me.

"Damn. That's too bad," Jimmy replied, his mouth turning down a little. "Seemed like the two of you really hit it off."

You have no idea how great we were together.

LATER, AFTER JIMMY AND EMILY HAD retired for the night, I showered and changed. Tired of being cooped up in my room, I slipped back downstairs and into the living room. Sitting in the armchair, I pulled out my cell and quickly tapped on the Chicago number.

"Hello?" a sleep-roughened voice answered.

"Hey, Eli. Sorry to wake you. It's Gunner."

"Hey, Gunner." Eli cleared his throat. "It's been a while."

After my squad and I had been discharged, we'd all gone back to our respective homes across the country, and we hadn't spoken since.

"Yeah, too long. I've been meaning to call, but you know how it is. Life got in the way. Anyway, the good thing is that I'm settling in New York City...at least for a while. How are things with you?"

"Eh," Eli answered, "I'm adjusting. There's a fair number of hybrid shifters around here in Chicago, so I've been learning a lot, though most of it has been the hard way and not without some danger. But, bigger than that, what are you doing in New York, bro?"

"I moved up here. Got a job as a security guard for a museum, and I'm staying with a friend until I can figure things out a bit more."

"I see." Eli paused. "Julia with you?"

"No. She didn't take it too well when I

showed her what I really was. So, we broke up."

"Man, I'm sorry. That shit has to be rough."

"Yeah, well." I was surprised to realize talking about Julia wasn't nearly as difficult as it used to be. "Shit happens. I've got bigger problems now."

"Oh, yeah? What did you run into? You stepped on someone's toes already?"

"Not exactly," I answered with a snort. "Have you ever met an actual pure-blooded wolf-shifter?"

"Sure, I know a few. Most of the shifters around here are jaguars, bears, and mountain lions. But wolf-shifters seem to be about as rare to the shifter community as we hybrids are to the supernatural community. What the hell were you doing with a pure-blooded shifter?"

"I had sex with her."

Eli laughed. "Oh, damn. Did you know she was a pureblood before you fucked her?"

"Yeah, I did. She told me, along with the fact that she'd never met a hybrid wolf-shifter before." I launched into the rest of the story, telling Eli about how we'd gotten a room and how I'd had a weird hallucination. "It was pretty crazy," I finished, shaking my head, remembering it all over again. "And she was gone before I could ask her about it."

"Did she experience the same thing?"

I shrugged. "I don't know. I fell asleep without asking her, and like I said, she was gone when I woke up. She did seem a little uncomfortable afterward, though. Come to think about it...maybe even a little freaked out about something. Although she told me everything was fine when I asked."

"Hmm." Eli was silent for a long while. "That's interesting because I thought she would have...except maybe..."

"What?" I snapped. Eli's mutterings were setting me on edge. "Spit it out, Eli."

"Gunner, what exactly do you know about this woman?"

"Not much," I admitted. "I spent most of today trying to track her down, but all I could find out from a few people I asked was that she's some rich guy's daughter." *This explained the free luxury room last night. Celine's father probably owned the place.*

"So, she didn't really tell you anything

about pure-blooded shifters other than the fact that she was one?"

"No. I mean, I know enough about them. Purebloods can change into their full beast, and we can't. Why? Is there something else I should know?"

Eli sighed. "Well, from what I understand, purebloods are different from us in a few other ways. I mean, apart from the fact that purebloods are born, not made, and unlike hybrids, they can actually get pregnant."

My jaw dropped. "Oh." *Shit. Thank God I used a condom.*

"And there's something else."

"What is it?" I replied impatiently.

"Those hallucinations you had? It sounds a hell of a lot like what my friend experienced when he found his true mate."

"His what?"

Eli sighed. "I have a buddy at work who happens to be a pure-blooded wolf-shifter. He was telling me about his wife and mentioned how lucky he was to have her because she was his true mate. Apparently, every pure-blooded shifter has one, but not very many ever find theirs. He said something about having a vision, and that was how he knew that she was the one. And that light show you were describing to me seems like it could have been something like that."

"But that doesn't make any sense," I protested. "Why would I have had a vision like that if I'm not a pureblood? Guadalupe never mentioned any of this true-mate shit to us."

"Look, man, I'm not an expert on any of this bullshit," Eli replied. "And maybe Guadalupe didn't mention any of that because, as far as I know, hybrids don't have true mates. Female hybrids can't even reproduce. But we can produce human offspring with a human female, and I'm guessing that means it wouldn't be pure-blooded with a shifter. I don't know why the fuck this is happening to you, man. I'm sorry. Besides, I'm probably totally off with my info."

"And why do you think that?"

"Because, normally, when purebloods find their true mate, they latch on and never let go. This woman practically ran out on you, right? Why the hell would she do that? Especially considering it's so hard for purebloods to actually find their true mates."

"I don't know," I admitted. "Maybe the

truth is that I was just hallucinating, and she had regrets or something and decided she had to get the hell out of there. I found out she's a rich guy's daughter, and after all, I'm..."

I'm fucking nobody right now because I haven't decided what the hell I want to be yet.

But the idea that Celine considered me a mistake hurt more than I cared to admit.

Shit. Maybe it was better this way. At least I wasn't being tied to a woman I hardly knew by a force I didn't quite understand.

"Yeah, well, I hope you're right, bro," Eli drawled and then yawned. "I've got to go now. I've only got a few hours left until I have to rise and shine, and I need to make the most of it. Call me if anything new comes up, all right?"

"Yeah, of course." I had forgotten that Eli worked an early-morning shift. "Thanks a lot, Eli. Talk to you later, bro."

Ending our call, I turned toward the kitchen and raised a brow at Emily, who was standing by the fridge, sipping something from a mug. I knew she'd been listening to most of my conversation. I hadn't heard her come down the stairs, but it wasn't exactly as if I could do more than glare at her since it was her damn house. I held her gaze for a few moments and then inclined my head before getting up and stomping upstairs and into my room.

The sooner I get out of this place, the better.

11

CELINE

I REPRESSED a sigh as I slid one leg out of the limousine and placed my stiletto heel onto the pavement. Reaching out my hand in a practiced move, I allowed the limousine driver to help me out of the vehicle, thanked him with a quiet murmur, and then turned to Carter, who held his arm out for me.

His eyes gleamed with lust as they roamed over my body, taking in the way my tight, curvy figure looked in the black sheath dress with a plunging neckline that I knew showed off my cleavage. Gold jewelry glittered at my ears, wrists, and neck—jewelry he'd purchased for me along with the dress and shoes he'd insisted I wear today. And I'd grudgingly done exactly as he'd requested.

So much for being wild and free.

My thoughts flashed back to Friday night when I'd been at the club—and more importantly, in Gunner's arms. I longed to be back there, dancing with Gunner, instead of here with Carter as I stood there, all coiffed and manicured to perfection. I felt like a damn porcelain doll—delicate, dainty, and unreal— meant to be put on a pedestal and admired by others. And not to be played with and certainly never expected to run around and do things on my own.

Some fucking shifter I am.

"Are you ready?" Carter asked politely, waiting for me to take his proffered arm.

Reluctantly, I turned my attention back to him. A light breeze teased the strands of his honey-blond hair, which was perfectly cut and styled. Standing at six foot three and muscular, he was classically handsome, but his eyes—the color of a pale Earl Grey tea— were cold in the afternoon sunshine, and his smile was razor-edged, letting me know he had not forgiven me. He'd caught lingering traces of Gunner's scent on me. Though he hadn't been able to prove I'd had sex with Gunner, I knew Carter suspected, and it chafed him because I'd yet to have sex with him.

Stupid, stupid, stupid. Why the hell did I fuck Gunner?

If I hadn't had sex with Gunner, I never would have known he was my true mate. And this terrible longing to be with him wouldn't afflict me. A longing I'd been fighting ever since I left him in the room yesterday morning.

"Yes," I responded while adjusting my silk wrap around my shoulders before placing my hand on his arm.

I bit back a sigh as we walked up the stairs and into the museum located in the heart of midtown Manhattan. The Museum of Modern Art was the last place I wanted to be. Having grown up in Manhattan, I'd been here often enough, and while I enjoyed art, I was no museum aficionado. But Carter was obsessed with sculptures. He was constantly having new ones made to decorate his loft apartment, and it was his turn to pick our date.

Not that I was actually allowed to pick

anything fun when it was my turn. I highly doubted he would consent to go to a R&B concert with me or to take me skydiving. Carter was far too serious and unadventurous. He was a stick-in-the-mud—a highly unusual trait for a shifter—which made me all the unluckier to have been paired with a straitlaced asswipe like him.

"After we've seen everything, I'll take you to the Met Rooftop Bar. We'll enjoy the view of Central Park with a glass of wine," Carter confessed. Though the only evidence of such excitement was the slight curling at the corners of his mouth. "I haven't visited the MoMA in a year, and I'm sure they've added more pieces since then."

Whoopee! Sounds like so much damn fun...not.

"That sounds lovely," I mumbled, careful to keep the sarcasm out of my voice.

I allowed Carter to lead me through the high-ceiling museum space, past the exhibits of paintings, photography, and architecture, and into the elevator.

"Visiting Vincent van Gogh's *Starry Night* today, sir?" the elevator operator asked politely as he closed behind us.

"Indeed," Carter answered, looking down

his nose at the man in a way that made me want to smack the self-important look off his damn face. "I don't suppose there are any new exhibits on display?"

"As a matter of fact, there are several," the elevator operator answered with considerably less candor as he pressed the button for the fifth floor. "The Collection galleries are frequently reinstalled in an effort to feature a wide range of artworks."

"Is that so?" Carter answered, his eyes lighting with real interest. His lips curled at the corners. "That is very pleasing news, indeed. Thank you."

We stepped out onto the fifth floor, and I tugged my white silk wrap a little closer around me as I looked around the gallery. We walked around the area to view the two Van Gogh paintings, a whole room of Monet, Picasso, and Matisse, while I listened to Carter drone on and on about the collections and the artistic value they brought to society. I supposed it might have been more interesting if he'd sounded more passionate about the subject. But the way he spoke about the pieces, I could tell he was more interested in them on an academic, maybe even fiscal, level, rather than as artistic pieces in and of themselves. But then, Carter was a ruthless businessman, and that was simply how he was. He didn't look at things and admire or enjoy them for what they were. He was always thinking and calculating as to how they could be more useful to him.

And, right now, with me being the sole heir to Cooper Enterprises, I was extremely useful to Carter.

The crowds around *Starry Night* were particularly large, but we worked our way to the front to admire it.

"Carter, could we please sit down for a moment?" I asked after a while when we found ourselves in an empty gallery. "I'm afraid I need to rest." I wasn't really tired. I just wanted a brief respite from his incessant, annoying chatter.

"Certainly," Carter agreed.

I didn't miss the flash of annoyance in his eyes. His grip tightened fractionally on my arm as he steered me to one of the few benches around, and a shiver ran up my spine. There was always a barely leashed violence lurking under the surface of his touch. He had a dominant alpha air that I knew probably thrilled and excited most women, but frankly, it unnerved me. I sat down on the bench and forced myself not to scoot away when he sat down too close next to me with his leg touching mine.

"Celine," Carter murmured, taking one of my hands in both of his. The warmth radiating off his body chased away some of the chill surrounding me, but it did absolutely nothing to put me at ease. "Have you given any more thought to our mating ceremony? I need it to happen soon. I've been a rather patient man."

"I..." I trailed off, the words stuck in my throat.

I knew I should just get this thing over with and go through with the mating ceremony, but the coldness in his voice and the violence that lurked beneath his icy-calm exterior always stopped me—as if, instinctively, I knew that this man, this shifter, was no good for me.

"I told you I'm not quite ready yet," I argued. "Just give me a little more time..."

"I have," he snarled, gripping my chin and tilting my head so that I looked up at him. "But I find myself growing a little impatient.

So impatient that I think I might contact my colleagues, advising them to start contacting their stockbrokers and begin liquidating assets." He blew out loudly. "I really don't understand why you insist on keeping me waiting."

I sucked in a breath as a jolt of real fear kicked up my pulse. Months ago, when he had first asked me to be his mate and I'd refused, Carter had told me he held a large portion of the company's stock under the names of a variety of shareholders in his network, and if I refused to be his mate, he would sell them all at once. I knew if he did that, it would mean utter disaster for Dad's company, Cooper Enterprises. The company's value would plummet drastically, and Carter would have absolutely no problem swooping in and buying the company for a fraction of its value, leaving Dad with absolutely nothing.

Shit. Think, Celine...fast.

I had always managed to hold Carter off, telling him I wouldn't be pushed into rash action and that, if he wanted me to marry him, he would have to give me time to get to know him better. The stall tactic had worked. Carter had risen to the challenge but with the caveat that, after another month, I would have to set a date for our ceremony to take place.

I thought of the many ways I could now handle his surging aggression. One, Superman-punch him in the damn throat for touching me in such a high-handed manner, or two, bide my time by soothing his savage beast and not ruffling his fur by going alpha female on his ass. Given his inflated ego and, more importantly, the leverage he had on Dad...I reluctantly went with option two.

"Release me now," I demanded before sliding my hand along the length of his arm and then wrapping my fingers around the wrist of the hand that held my chin immobile.

He hesitated and then obeyed.

Taking a soothing deep breath, I paused before continuing, "And, as far as my request for you to wait—" I shrugged "—I am a woman, and it is in our nature to make a man wait. Besides, don't you find that it heightens the anticipation and makes the reward more...pleasurable?" I deliberately uttered the last word in a husky sex-kitten manner.

"Vixen," he growled, wrapping his free arm around my waist and drawing me closer.

I sucked in another breath of revulsion but tried to pass it off as a breathy moan instead.

I fucking despise him, my wolf complained. *Please let me disembowel him and let us be done with him.*

No, I snapped back while pulling my inner cage firmly around her.

"Celine, you are playing with fire," Carter hissed. Leaning in, he caught my earlobe between his teeth.

My inner beast snarled and stomped around in protest. I shivered with distaste, finding it hard to resist the impulse to squirm away from him—or better yet, hurl.

"Excuse me," a familiar deep voice interrupted.

I jerked my head up in shock. Gunner stood there, dressed in a dark suit with a matching tie and starched white shirt. His hands were clasped loosely in front of him, and I caught a glimpse of what looked like a radio communicator and a bottle of Mace hanging from the belt beneath his suit jacket.

"I'll have to ask the two of you to move along."

His silver-gray eyes had morphed to cold steel, and he showed absolutely no recognition on his features, which hurt like a motherfucker, though I knew it was obviously better for both of us that he showed no hint that we knew each other.

"I beg your pardon," Carter snapped, slowly removing his hands from my body. "Do you have any inkling of who I am?"

Gunner blankly stared at him.

"Well, I have been a benefactor of this museum since—" Carter stopped cold, his nose twitching as he sniffed the air. "It's you!" he snarled before his eyes turned bright gold and he whirled on me.

I sprang back while my inner wolf yelled, *Celine, quick! Go for his throat and rip it out!*

"This filth is the man you were with?" Carter jeered.

Before I could stop him, Carter launched himself at Gunner, going in for the kill.

GUNNER

"JESUS CHRIST, Gunner. What the hell were you thinking?" Jimmy asked.

Biting back a groan, I pinched the bridge of my nose and closed my eyes, willing my headache to ease. My head had been smashed into the wall, hard enough that it would have cracked my skull open if I were only human. But, even now, I wasn't fully healed yet. I was in Jimmy's car while he drove us home from the police station where I'd been questioned at great length before being released. And all I wanted right now was to get to my bedroom and forget about this whole horrible day.

"Bro," I answered, "it wasn't my fault. He attacked me."

"For no reason?" Jimmy asked incredulously. "That's going to be hard to convince the boss of."

I sighed. "No, it wasn't for no reason," I corrected, leaning my head back against the headrest. My headache was beginning to fade a little, to my damn relief. I was just happy to be heading home after this whole clusterfuck. "He was pissed because I'd fucked his girlfriend."

Well, I guess that explains why Celine ran out on me the next morning.

It was just my luck that the first woman I had sex with in the months since Julia happened to not only belong to another man, but a man who was a generous and very wealthy benefactor of my employer.

"What are you talking about?" Jimmy asked.

I quickly gave him a rundown about what had led up to the altercation.

Jimmy's jaw dropped. "So, let me get this straight. You two were fighting over the same woman you'd picked up in the bar the other night?"

"Her name is Celine. And, yes, the very same. Only I had no clue she wasn't single, and I damn sure wasn't expecting to see her again." Even though I had wanted to.

I'd hardly recognized Celine, given the fact that she was decked out in that expensive-looking black dress and wrap with her hair twisted into an elegant updo. The whole ensemble had made her look way different from the other night. But I'd instantly recognized her scent, and when I had seen her sitting next to that man, letting him paw her, a strange, possessive streak had taken hold of me. I couldn't stop myself from butting in. Truth be told, I could fully understand why the bastard had attacked me. Every instinct in me had longed to rip his throat out because of the way he had been touching Celine. My inner beast had wanted blood because another man was touching what was...his—Celine.

"Shit. But to find her again, and with another man...damn...you have the worst luck ever."

"Apparently so."

"I guess we all run that risk when it comes to hooking up with strangers," Jimmy countered. "Shit. I should be grateful I don't have to worry about that crap anymore," he added with a weak laugh.

"Yeah," I muttered. "Lucky you."

Jimmy winced. "Shit. Sorry. Forgot about the whole thing with Julia. Fuck. I'm being pretty insensitive, aren't I?"

"Don't worry about it," I answered, looking out the window to catch a glimpse of the afternoon sun before we pulled up to Jimmy's house and parked. "I'm happy for you."

"Mark my words, Gunner. You'll come through all this shit," Jimmy said as we hopped out of the vehicle. "And I'll personally speak to the boss and try to help round up some witness statements for you. But I have a feeling luck is on your side. I mean, just look at you," he muttered, making a sweeping motion across my body. "There's hardly a scratch on you even though you told me that the bastard had plowed you straight into the damn wall. Shit. If it weren't for your clothes, I'd find it hard to believe you were even in a fight."

I chuckled, looking down at myself. My suit jacket was torn at the elbow, and there were tears in my pants and scuffs all over my shiny new boots. "Wasn't exactly expecting to spend my first paycheck on getting a new suit," I grumbled, stomping up the stairs into the house. I knew Jimmy was trying to cheer me up, but right now, my stomach was churning with way too many raw emotions—anger, frustration, bitterness, envy, and confusion. "I'll be in my room if you need me."

Back in my bedroom, I stripped off my ruined clothes and changed into a pair of jeans and a T-shirt, not bothering to clean up in the bathroom. My stomach continued to roil unpleasantly with anxiety and rage, and I wished like hell for some kind of outlet on which to vent my surging emotions.

Shit. I can't believe Celine played me like this.

She was clearly involved with another of her own kind. I couldn't imagine that pure-blooded wolf-shifters were any less territorial than hybrids, and it was obvious that Carter Langstrom—as I'd learned my attacker was named—was a powerful man. Now, it was highly likely I would lose my job, and then all of my hard work over the past few weeks would be for damn nothing.

"Gunner?" Emily knocked on the door,

and for once, there was no hint of disapproval in her voice. "There's a visitor here to see you."

Scowling, I opened the door. "Who is it?" I asked wearily.

She eyed me carefully. "I think you ought to see for yourself."

Sighing in exasperation, I followed her down the steps and into the living room. I stopped short at the sight of Celine standing just inside the front door, clutching her handbag in both hands and biting down on her lower lip.

She straightened when she saw me, but I noticed her death grip on her bag. Subdued and obviously nervous, she bore little resemblance to the feisty, confident, and sexy vixen who'd beguiled me back at the club. Yet my heart ached at the sight of her. I longed to pull her into my arms and smooth the lines of stress from her face.

Instead, my jaw tightened as I stood at the foot of the stairs. "How did you find me, Celine?"

She smiled faintly. "You can do a lot with a name and place of employment, Mr. Norcross." She cleared her throat. "I'd like a few minutes of your time, if you wouldn't mind."

She's so damn stiff. So formal. Who the hell is this woman? And what did she do with the real Celine?

"I don't think so," I grunted. "You need to leave."

"Gunner!" Emily scolded, giving me a reproachful glare. "How incredibly rude." She turned to Celine with a warm smile, catching me off guard. "Why don't you have a seat? And I'll get you a cup of tea."

She bustled off before I could say a word, and I gaped after her, openmouthed.

Doesn't she know that Celine is a wolf-shifter? And why the hell is she being so nice to her?

She should be railing at me for bringing the trouble she'd warned me about into her house and threatening to kick me to the curb.

"So, are you just going to completely ignore me?" Celine inquired.

I turned to stare at her. She was now perched on one of the love seats, her back straight and her hands folded neatly on her lap, but a glimmer of heat in her eyes told me that the woman who'd turned me inside out on Friday night wasn't completely lost and buried within the elegant, refined socialite who sat before me now.

"I haven't exactly come here without risk to myself, you know," she finished.

I ignored her words. "Where is your boyfriend?" I asked abruptly, glancing over to the window.

If Carter followed her here...I would beat his ass like he stole something.

I sighed heavily. But I couldn't let Jimmy or Emily get caught up in all of this dramatic, reality show bullshit.

"Carter is meeting with his lawyers now," Celine confessed stiffly. She glanced toward the kitchen, lowering her voice. "Do you think there's somewhere more...private we can speak?"

I scoured her face for any hint of an ulterior motive, but I couldn't find one. I had to admit, this wasn't a conversation I wanted Emily to overhear. Nor did I want Jimmy walking in to find Celine sitting on his couch when he returned home. He'd gone back to work as soon as he dropped me off. And I didn't know why Emily was so keen for me to talk to Celine, but it was clear she wasn't going to allow me to kick Celine the fuck out until we talked, so I simply nodded tersely and led her upstairs to my room.

"So, this is where you spend most of your time?" she asked, sitting on the edge of my mattress as I closed the door behind us.

It did strange, unspeakable things to my insides to see her sitting on my bed. I fought the urge to push her back onto the sheets to see if round two would be just as mind-blowing as the other night.

But I thought better of it.

"When I'm not working, yeah." I crossed over to the wall opposite the foot of the bed and leaned against it, tucking my body into the corner. The more distance I could put between us, the better. "Figured that going out would only get me into trouble. Guess I was right." I gave her a pointed look.

She dropped her eyes. "I'm sorry about that," she stated quietly, fisting her hands in her lap.

Her fingernails had been repainted a pale pink, I noticed, one that suited her current look much better than the fiery red talons she'd scored my back with while she screamed my name over and over.

"You told me you were visiting from out of town, so I thought it would be safe. If I'd known you actually lived here…"

"You would have found another tourist to cheat on your boyfriend with?" I asked sharply.

She jerked her chin up.

"Well, I feel so much better about that shit," I continued, sarcasm dripping from every word.

Her eyes narrowed. "Carter's not my boyfriend," she snapped, clenching her fists. "And for the record, I don't just run around town, having sex with guys."

"Oh, so I'm a special case, then?" I rolled my eyes. I wasn't buying this sweet and innocent act for a second. "That's great to know. So, if the guy who nearly ripped my throat out today wasn't your boyfriend, then what exactly is he? The protector of your damn virtue?"

"Don't be ridiculous," Celine snapped, her proper demeanor slipping. "He's…well, I guess you could say he's my fiancé…sort of."

I threw up my hands. "This is bullshit! That asshole is your fiancé!" It was a statement, not a question. "That shit is even worse than being your boyfriend. I had a one-night stand with the fiancée of one of MoMA's primary benefactors twenty-four hours before my first real day of work. Fuck! Lady Fate really knows how to play her cards."

"He's not my fiancé!" Celine shouted as she came off the bed, rapidly closing the distance between us. Catching herself, she backed up a pace and added more quietly, "Although I promised myself to him...the shit is...complicated."

I snorted. "So, he's not your boyfriend. And he's not your fiancé," I answered. My emotions were warring between the desire to strangle her or pull her close to me. "Can you please tell me why the hell you're explaining all this and why I should even give a shit?"

Celine ran a hand through her hair, causing some of her dark curls to spill free from her carefully styled updo. My fingers twitched, wanting to run my hands through her tresses, but I curled them into fists at my sides instead.

"The truth is, I don't want to marry him. But if I don't, he's going to destroy my dad's company, and he'll lose everything." Her voice dropped to a whisper, and her eyes were fixed on a square of carpet near my left foot. "Friday night was just supposed to be one last night of freedom before I gave myself over to Carter. I never expected to meet you or for it to turn out like this."

Anger surged through me, though for a change, it wasn't directed at Celine but at the man who was manipulating her. "How the hell is he going to destroy your father's company?"

Celine sighed. "Carter owns a great deal of our stock, which is being held for him by a large number of different people scattered across the globe. If I don't agree to marry him, he'll sell it all, and my dad's company value will drop drastically."

"But that shit is blackmail," I protested. "Surely, you can just report something like this to the police, can't you?"

"No." She shook her head. "Carter is too damn powerful. The authorities wouldn't be able to take direct action against him without something more substantial than my word. I hired a private investigator about a month ago to look into Carter, but so far, he hasn't been able to find anything tangible we can use. Carter's just too good at covering his tracks."

"Damn." I clenched my fists. "I wish there were something I could do to help you."

Celine smiled faintly. "It's not your problem to solve," she muttered. "And I've done enough damage by putting you on Carter's radar. Gunner...I just came by to apologize for what I did. And to tell you that I'll make sure Carter steers clear of you. You don't deserve all the drama involved with my problems."

Her apology should have made me feel better. Instead, I felt helpless and like shit.

"You don't have to apologize for anything," I insisted. "None of this is your fault, and you're dealing with it a lot better than most women I know would be."

"But..."

Whatever she was going to say was cut off as I gathered her up into my arms and kissed her, drowning in her sweet scent and taste. She moaned, her arms tightening around me, and relief spread through me because she was finally back in my arms. Then, lust that was so powerful ripped through me, and I nearly backed her onto the bed and stripped her clothes off.

What is it about this woman that makes me feel so damn hungry? So damn possessive? Shit. I'd never felt this way about anyone before, not even Julia.

"I spent all yesterday looking for you," I confessed, breaking the kiss so I could stare down at her. "I haven't been able to get you out of my head, and I don't understand why."

I bent my head down to kiss her again, but this time, she turned her head away, so my mouth landed on her cheek.

"Gunner...we shouldn't do this."

"Why not?" I murmured, trailing kisses across her jawline and down the graceful column of her neck.

Her voice barely penetrated through the fog of lust clouding my brain. And, damn, she smelled so good. All I could think of was having more of her in any position I could possibly get her into.

"I..." Her breath caught as I pushed up her skirt, sliding my hand underneath.

My cock hardened as my fingers brushed against her wet panties. The smell of her arousal was pleasing and heady.

Wasting no time, I slipped my hand beneath the waistband of her panties to touch her. "Just tell me you don't want me, and I'll stop."

Another moan escaped her lips, and I was about to slip a finger inside her tight cunt.

"Gunner, stop," she sobbed, her body trembling in my arms.

I snatched my hand back as though her pussy had scalded me.

Celine took the opportunity to put some distance between us, her eyes glowing and her chest heaving. "I can't do this. If Carter smells you on me, he'll know where I've been, and there's no telling what he'll do."

"Fuck," I growled. "You have to leave. If you don't, I can't be responsible for what happens next."

Celine nodded and fixed her hair before moving toward the door. Gritting my teeth, I fought the compulsion to catch her by the wrist, to drag her back into my arms and never, ever let her go. The urge was ridiculously strong and confused the shit out of me.

"Celine..." I began.

She paused, one foot already across the threshold.

"I talked to a friend about what happened between us on Friday night. So, tell me the truth. Am I your true mate?"

She slowly turned her head to look at me, and my heart stuttered at the tears running down her cheeks.

"Yes," she croaked in an achingly soft whisper. "And I'm so sorry that I did this to you."

And then she was gone...out of my bedroom and out of my life forever.

❧ 13 ❧

CELINE

"Celine? Darling, what's wrong?" Carter inquired.

Closing my eyes, I polished off the wine in my glass and then lowered it as I stared across the limousine interior to where Carter was reclined, his eyes glimmering in the darkness.

"Nothing," I answered before crossing my legs and trying to assume a languid pose of my own. "Why do you ask?"

"Well, that's your fifth glass of wine tonight," Carter pointed out, raising an eyebrow as he glanced to my empty glass. "I don't usually see you drink so much."

My lips curved into a smile that I knew

didn't reach my eyes. "It's simply cold out tonight, and the wine keeps me warm."

"You're chilly? Why didn't you just say so?" Leaning over, Carter pressed a button on the wall, and the privacy screen between the driver and us slid down. "Jared, please turn up the heat."

"Yes, sir." The privacy screen rose again, and the warm air issuing from the air vents suddenly intensified. "Is that better?"

"Yes, thank you."

I bit my lip, looking out the window and wishing I hadn't spoken at all, as the interior of the car quickly grew stuffy. It didn't help when Carter leaned across the space between us and took my left hand into his.

"I'm so happy you finally agreed to set a date for our mating ceremony," he murmured, rubbing the pad of his thumb across the yellow princess-cut diamond that glimmered on my ring finger. "The ring looks absolutely stunning on you."

My pulse jumped—not in lust, but in anger. "Apparently. I've gotten many compliments on it," I replied, struggling against the urge to withdraw my hand from his and wiping any trace of his touch on my clothes.

"As you should." He grinned devilishly.

The fucker was enjoying tormenting me. I knew he was relishing the fact that he now held me submissive to him, especially when I desired to be anything but.

"And I've also received lots of well wishes and congratulations," I concluded.

"We are, after all, the perfect pair."

He brushed his lips against my skin, and a shiver of revulsion rippled up my spine. I'd thought I'd gotten used to the feel of his skin against mine, but ever since I'd slept with Gunner, I'd hardly been able to tolerate Carter's touch. My inner wolf and my body instinctively screamed out against the wrongness of someone other than my true mate—Gunner—touching me. But there was nothing I could do about it.

Carter practically owned me now...body and soul.

We pulled up to Carter's building in the bustling Financial District located in the Seaport area of Manhattan. I'd been here only once before with him, before he'd first proposed to me. Back then, we'd taken his yacht out for the day and then come back to his place to enjoy dinner on his terrace while watching the sun set over the horizon.

Strange, how an incredibly romantic setting can feel so wrong when you're with someone you don't even like.

We both stepped out of the limo, and I took his arm, allowing him to lead me into the building, then the elevator. Once we'd arrived on his floor, we entered into his full-floor, designer loft apartment. It was much the same as it had been the last time I was there. Casually, I glanced around the living room as Carter took my coat. Everything in his place was done in black and white, from white leather furniture to the black lacquered coffee and side tables, seamlessly blending in with the black marble floors. It suited Carter's personality perfectly. He was gloom and doom.

"Why don't you sit down?" he suggested, bringing me a glass of red wine. "I'll just go ahead and fetch your gift."

I did as he'd suggested, trying not to allow the wine glass to shake in my hand as I brought it to my lips. I knew I'd never hear the end of it if I spilled one drop on Carter's pristine couch. Looking out the bay window behind the dining room table on the other side of the room, I tried not to cringe in apprehension of what his gift might be. Over dinner, Carter had told me he'd bought me something but that he wanted to give it to me at his apartment. This was the sole reason I hadn't been able to simply beg off from even coming here, going to my own home afterward.

The tapping of his footsteps on the floor drew my attention away from the view, and I turned to see Carter approaching me with a long, expensive-looking black box in his hand. The kind that trendy, upscale boutiques used to gift wrap clothing in.

Shit.

Dread pooled in my belly at the broad smile on his face, and I hesitantly took the box from him.

"Well?" He loomed over me, clearly not willing to let me deliberate. "Aren't you going to open it?"

Carefully, I removed the box lid and set it aside. Then I lifted a lacy black negligee from the gold tissue paper. The fabric was sheer along the stomach and where my nipples

would show, and pale pink flowers were em-
broidered along the bust and the hem.

"I'm not entirely sure this gift is for me,"
I remarked slowly, barely holding back the
rage that wanted to suffuse my voice.

Rip it to shreds! my beast demanded. *Who
does this asshole think he is, buying us something
so...inappropriate? We don't even want him.*

I sighed heavily. Resigned to my fate, I
replied back to my inner wolf, *It's perfectly
normal for a man to buy a woman he's dating lingerie. Particularly if that man and woman are
engaged.*

This is utter nonsense, my wolf shrieked. *I
want Gunner.*

"This gift is for both of us," he drawled. His
smile widened in clear anticipation. "Why don't
you go ahead and try it on for me? I'll wait right
here." He settled himself in the armchair near
the fireplace with an expectant look on his face.

Biting back the urge to throw the gar-
ment and the box in his face, I decided to
bite the bullet and not protest. This was my
life now, after all. I was his, and we were to
be married.

Quietly, I rose to my feet and headed to

the hall bathroom. Inside, I found the negligee wasn't the only thing in the box. There was also a pair of sheer thigh-high stockings and matching garters with a garter belt.

Oh, for fuck's sake. He wants me to dress up like some simpering sex kitten?

Gritting my teeth, I undressed and donned the garments, knowing full well that Carter planned to do a lot more tonight than admire me in this sexy getup.

Well...I knew that this day would come eventually.

I had dodged having sex with him for as long as I could.

All righty. Best to get this fuckfest started and over with quickly rather than draw this shit out.

Completely dressed, I glanced in the mirror and debated on whether or not I should wear my hair loose or keep it pinned up as it was now. My hair would look like a wild, wanton mess when it was down, which was exactly the opposite of the proper young socialite I forced myself to be for Carter. I also knew Carter was a total control freak and would welcome any show of my rebellious streak, only so he could crush it like a bug. So, I decided to leave my hair as it was.

Taking a deep breath, I stepped out of the bathroom and returned to the living room. Carter was sprawled on the couch with his arms resting on the backs of the cushions. He sat up a little straighter, a slow, appreciative smile spreading across his face.

"You look just as I imagined you would," he whispered as he held his arms out to me. "Come to me, my mate."

Mate? My inner wolf shrilled. *He's not our mate. This is bullshit.*

Slowly, I put one foot in front of the other, suppressing the impulse to run in the opposite direction, like the hounds of hells were nipping at my heels.

Carter was relaxed and welcoming right now, but I knew that could change in a moment. In the blink of an eye, I'd seen his rage surface at the smallest of infractions. Trembling, I stopped just in front of him, my shins barely touching his knees.

"There you are," he whispered, settling his hands around my waist and yanking me forward. "Come, sit on top of me."

Take a damn deep breath, Celine, and just jump into the pit of hell.

I straddled his hips and tried not to flinch

as he rubbed his repulsive erection between my legs.

Oh my God, this is really happening.

Panic choked off my air. Every muscle in my body tightened as he gripped the back of my head with his right hand, hard enough to hurt, bringing my lips down to meet his in a bruising kiss. Bile rose in my throat, and I fought the urge to throw up into his mouth.

"Are you ready?" he murmured against my mouth, his cigar-laced breath sending shivers of revulsion down my spine.

I nodded stiffly.

"You seem a little...tense," he remarked while digging his fingers into my shoulders with force.

I knew that, if I were human, he would have left marks on my skin.

"It's our first time. I'm...just a little nervous," I babbled.

Taking a deep breath, I consciously willed my muscles to relax. It didn't help that my inner beast was staging a one-woman revolt by running around in circles, snarling and growling obscenities.

Maybe if I could get my body language to

stop screaming no, he would be gentler with me.

"I don't want to disappoint you," I whispered.

"Oh, don't worry, darling," he said as his grip eased on my shoulders. "I'm sure you will please me very much." He began trailing kisses down my jawline and throat, much in the same way that Gunner had done to me. "It will make things...easier for you if you do."

Gunner. My pulse quickened a little. *Just think of Gunner. Everything will be fine if I just picture his smoking-hot body.*

Closing my eyes so I didn't have to see Carter's blond hair and pale brown eyes, I allowed the fantasy to form in my mind that it was Gunner I was straddling. Gunner was sliding his fingers into my hair, pressing kisses against my skin. A tiny moan escaped my lips as he began nibbling on my collarbone, teasing the sensitive skin there.

"Mmm, I can smell your arousal. Do you want me, Celine?"

The sound of Carter's voice threatened to shatter my hot fantasy, and I squeezed my eyes tighter, holding on to the image of Gunner's tousled dark hair and swirling silver eyes.

Damn. I could get lost in those gorgeous eyes forever, caught up in their intensity, while drowning in my lust for him.

Yes. Gunner.

Desire came flooding through me like an ocean.

"Yes," I breathed. "Yes, please."

"All in due time." His hands slid up my torso to cup my full breasts, and he pinched my nipples roughly.

I cried out at the pleasure and pain, all while losing myself in the memory of Gunner circling his muscular arms around my waist, bringing my chest forward so he could capture my nipple with his mouth.

Damn...his tongue feels so good...

"Gunner," I moaned, clutching at his head as he sucked on my taut bud.

Carter stilled beneath my hands. "What did you say?"

My eyes flew open. My breath left me in a rush as I saw Carter glaring at me. His eyes were bright with rage, his mouth compressed into a thin line.

Shit. Shit. Shit.

"Carter, I didn't—"

Pain exploded through my right cheek as he backhanded me, and I toppled off his lap and onto the floor.

"How dare you say his name to me!" he shouted, jumping to his feet. "How dare you think about another man while I'm making love to you. You'll pay for this, you little bitch," he growled, advancing on me.

I scooted back across the floor. "No!" I shouted. "I'm not taking your shit anymore." Shaking with anger and adrenaline, I scrambled to my feet. My claws and fangs extended, magnifying the pain of my cheekbone that he'd broken, but I ignored the agony, intent on my enemy.

"Fuck you, Carter. I'm a strong, independent woman, you bastard, and I won't be treated like your damn little mouse anymore."

Carter's body was massive compared to mine, but I didn't give a shit if I died defending myself.

Half-shifted, I sprang at him, my claws raking across the lower half of his face. He sidestepped before I could move in and sink my fangs into his throat. Carter grabbed my arm and flipped me onto my back, and my head knocked against the floor. Stars swam in my vision as I tried to struggle to my feet, but he was quickly on top of me, raining brutal blows down on my face and body, and it was all I could do to keep my arms up and try to block the worst of it.

"Fuck you! I will never be yours," I half sobbed, half snarled.

Blindly, I fought back with every ounce of my will. It was the last thing I remembered before I blacked out from the pain of him beating the shit out of me.

❧ 14 ❧

GUNNER

COOPER AND LANGSTROM Enterprises to Join Together as One Big Conglomerate in Holy Matrimony, the headline read as I opened up the evening paper.

Sighing in disgust, I resisted the urge to toss the paper and instead flipped to the next section. It had been two weeks since Celine and I last spoke. Two weeks since she and Carter had officially announced their engagement, and the press was still going on about it.

"Rough day?"

I looked up as Emily entered the kitchen, and I lowered the paper to the kitchen table, obscuring the headline so I wouldn't have to see the flash of pity in her eyes. She'd been remarkably more subdued in her dislike of me ever since Celine had come to the house, and I wondered just how much of the situation she'd managed to figure out. I'd refused to speak of the incident to anyone, and Emily had never asked, so I had no idea what she knew.

"Not really," I answered truthfully. "Just didn't get too much sleep last night."

I'd managed to keep my job at MoMA by the skin of my teeth but not without a little help from Jimmy—and, I suspected, interference from Celine. And, though I was walking on a tighter leash, it had been pretty smooth sailing so far.

Emily nodded. "Well, I've observed some distressing changes to your aura lately," she commented, turning her back to me as she rummaged through the refrigerator for ingredients to start dinner. "I imagine, if you could let out all that stress and negativity inside you, you might start to sleep better at night."

"Thanks for the advice, Doc," I retorted.

Emily turned toward me, a frown on her

face, but before she could say anything more, the phone rang.

"Excuse me," she said, placing a bundle of carrots on the counter and rushing from the room.

Not interested in hearing Emily chat with one of her Wiccan friends, I picked up the paper again and started perusing the Sports section. Then I froze as my keen hearing recognized the voice that spoke over the phone.

"Is Gunner Norcross available?" The female voice was shaky but unmistakably Celine's, and my sensitive hearing picked it up as clearly as if my ear were pressed to the phone.

"I can see if he's available," Emily answered. "Who can I say is calling?"

"Tell him it's Celine," she offered, "and that it's urgent."

"One moment." I heard Emily put down the phone, and a few seconds later, she entered the kitchen again. "I assume you heard all of that?"

I nodded, not looking up from the paper. "Why don't you take a message?"

I jerked as Emily snatched the paper

from my hands, and I looked up in surprise to see a thunderous scowl on her face.

"Why are you doing this?" she snapped, hands on her hips. "She obviously needs you."

"She can go to her fiancé for whatever she needs," I spat while getting to my feet before stomping out of the kitchen and up the stairs.

What the hell does Emily know about what's really going on between us anyway?

Celine was the one who had told me her problems weren't mine to solve. But just as I reached the top of the stairs, I heard a sob. One that had come from the other end of the line. The pain-ridden sound tugged at my heartstrings, and with a curse, I bounded back down the stairs and picked up the phone.

"Celine?"

"Gunner," Celine choked out. "Please, I can't walk, and I need your help. I'm down by the South Street Seaport—"

"Can't walk?" I interrupted, cold dread freezing my insides. "What the hell do you mean, you can't walk? Did you get into an accident?"

"No, I..." Celine took a shuddering

breath. "It's Carter. I just need to get the fuck away. Gunner, please help me."

Red filled my vision at the mention of that bastard's name, and my brain clicked as I put two and two together.

That fucker hurt my mate.

I memorized the information as she rattled off her location. "Stay there," I barked. "I'm on my way."

I hung up the phone with bloodlust coursing through my veins. *If I ever get my hands on that asshole, Carter...I'll fucking kill him.*

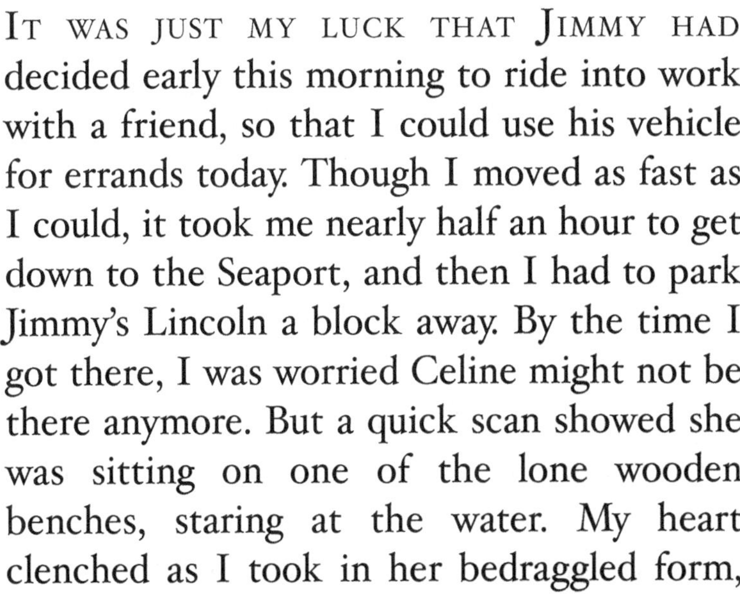

IT WAS JUST MY LUCK THAT JIMMY HAD decided early this morning to ride into work with a friend, so that I could use his vehicle for errands today. Though I moved as fast as I could, it took me nearly half an hour to get down to the Seaport, and then I had to park Jimmy's Lincoln a block away. By the time I got there, I was worried Celine might not be there anymore. But a quick scan showed she was sitting on one of the lone wooden benches, staring at the water. My heart clenched as I took in her bedraggled form, which was hunched and bundled inside her coat.

I stormed over to her. "Celine." I sank to my knees and gathered her into my arms before I could think better of it. "What the hell happened?"

"I fought back," Celine muttered through cracked, bloody lips, looking up at me out of eyes that were surrounded by swollen, purple skin. Her slender fingers curled into the fabric of my coat with a surprisingly strong grip. "I finally had enough of Carter's shit, and I fought back."

"Carter?" I could smell that bastard Carter's scent all over her. "That son of a bitch!"

A man hitting a woman was a punk move, but to touch my mate...that immediately put him on my fucking kill-on-sight list.

"Please...I don't want to talk about it right now." Celine buried her face into my shoulder. "I just need some time to figure things out. Can you take me home? Please?"

"Of course." I soothed her, stroking her back, though I had no idea where *home* was.

Does she live with her father?

Because, if so, I wasn't really sure I

wanted to be around for the conversation that was bound to ensue if I brought her home, looking like this. Yet there wasn't really any other option.

"Can you walk?"

"Yes. I think so," she whispered.

Struggling to get to her feet, she hunched over in pain again. Swiftly, I swung her up into my arms before she could collapse onto the pier.

"Jesus, he really fucked you up." I was trembling with rage. My hands were shaking so hard I had to force myself to stop so as not to further agitate Celine. Cradling her against my body, I walked back to the parking garage, ignoring the stares from the few people out on the streets at this time of night.

"I've already healed a lot," Celine rasped. "Just need you to wrap my ribs. I'll be fine in a few hours."

I gently laid her out across the back seat of the Lincoln and strapped myself into the driver's seat.

"Where am I taking you?" I asked. She rattled off an address that I entered into my GPS before I maneuvered out of the parking garage. "Okay, Celine. Rest, I'll take it from here."

"Thanks, Gunner." Her voice sounded strained.

I remained quiet for the rest of the twenty minutes it took me to wrestle through traffic to get there.

Finally approaching her tree-lined townhouse only a few steps from Central Park, I parked. The block was eerily quiet. Most of the homes looked uninhabited or under construction.

"I don't have many neighbors." Her voice sounded a little stronger, which was a good sign. "Most of these townhomes were purchased, gutted, and are now under renovation."

I came around to help Celine out. She took my hand and allowed me to help her to her feet. Unlike before, she was able to walk to the door, though she was still a little hunched over and had to cling to my arm for support. Muttering under her breath, she fished her keys from the pocket of the coat she wore and then fumbled with them for a few moments until she was able to open it.

Bright, bold colors and geometric designs

were the first impressions I got as I stepped into an open living space that was mostly dominated by the living room, with a dining table and chair set closest to me and a kitchen off to the right. I heard a sigh of relief from Celine as she closed the door behind me, and I led her to the turquoise-blue couch, gently but firmly settling her down onto it and tossing the bright yellow throw blanket lying over the back onto her.

"I'm starting to feel a bit better now," she announced, smiling weakly at me as I brushed a curl from her face.

"Yeah, you're healing up," I concluded, allowing my touch to linger against her cheek for a moment.

Her skin was so soft, so warm, and I just wanted to gather her into my arms and never let her go again.

No. Bad idea. Time to put some distance between the two of us.

But I chose to ignore my inner voice, and my hand moved to the top button of her coat. "We should get this off," I told her, "so I can check your injuries."

Celine seized my hand. "Don't," she cautioned, her voice strained.

I stilled. "Why? Don't you want to get this coat off you?"

"More than anything," she hissed. Then shame filled her eyes again, and she looked away. "I just...I just don't want you to see me like this," she whispered.

"Celine. I know how you must be feeling, but I really do need to make sure you're all right. I promise, it's okay."

I brushed my lips across her forehead, and after a long moment, she nodded.

Despite my promise, it took a lot of restraint not to lash out at something or break into a rant after I removed the coat and saw the half-shredded lingerie beneath. It didn't take a genius to figure out what had gone down. Taking a deep breath to steady my shaking hands, I ran my hands and eyes over her body, checking for anything out of the ordinary, but there was nothing other than some fading bruises around her ribs and some dried blood that had congealed around healing scratches that were no more than pink lines.

"Wh—" I choked and stopped myself. Clearing my throat, I continued, "Why did he do this to you?"

Celine turned her face away. "I don't want to talk about it," she whispered.

"Has he done this before?" I demanded, unable to keep the heat from my voice. "Is this how he gets off? By making you a little black and blue before he fucks you?"

"He's never, ever fucked me!" Celine yelled as she reared up, hands balled into fists. Her irises were tinged with a glowing gold band. "I've never let him get as close as he did tonight," she insisted more quietly now. "I said something that made him angry, and the two of us came to blows. It ended badly...for me, but I'm happy I was able to stand up for myself—finally. I blacked out somehow and woke up to find myself on the floor and Carter nowhere in sight. Thank God." She paused. "In spite of the pain, I knew I had to get the hell out of there before he came back. So, I grabbed my coat, shoes, cell, and keys and hightailed it out of his house. Confused and in pain, I limped around a little aimlessly before I got my shit together enough to think about calling a car service to pick me up... But look at me." She gestured to herself. "I'm a damn hot mess, and I didn't want some strange driver picking me up and recognizing me as the daughter of billionaire Damon Cooper and then snitching me out to the press. So, that's when I decided to call you."

"Jesus." I ran a hand through my hair and sighed. "I'm sorry. I shouldn't have reacted like that. I'm glad you were able to stand up for yourself. I just wish—"

"That I hadn't gotten hurt," Celine interjected, placing her hand atop mine. "I know."

We sat there for some time, my arm wrapped around her, as I tried hard to make her feel safe.

It seemed like forever before I finally broke the silence. "Is your fridge stocked?" I demanded, withdrawing my hand from beneath hers and rising to my feet. "I want to get some food into you. It will help you heal faster."

"There should be some stuff in the freezer," she replied, struggling to get to her feet.

"Okay. Just rest." I caught her by the arm, lowering her back down to the sofa. "I'll be right back."

She shook her head. "I just need to get out of these..." She gestured helplessly to the rags she was wearing, biting her lip. "Get the stench of him off me."

"Of course." I could have kicked myself.

It made sense that she wanted to get out of the shredded lingerie and remove any trace of his scent. If I hadn't been so rattled, I would have suggested it myself already.

"Do you need help?"

"I can do it." She smiled faintly. "I'll be out in a few."

An hour later, we were sitting at the dining table, steadily working our way through the pile of medium-rare hamburgers I had fried up.

"These aren't half bad," Celine said around a mouthful of what had to be her third burger, sounding a bit more like her old self. "Did you work as a short-order cook or something?"

"As a matter of fact, I worked part time at the campus café when I was in college," I admitted with a wink. "Coeds flocked from every corner of the campus for a taste of my chili-cheese fries!"

Celine laughed, a sound of genuine humor, warming me. She looked more like the old Celine now, dressed in a black tee printed with the slogan "Black Magic" in a distinctive gothic typeface and a pair of black yoga pants. Her wild curls were still a little damp from her shower and cascaded freely over her shoulders. There was healthy color in her cheeks.

"What did you study in college?" she asked, picking up a hamburger bun and slathering it with ketchup and mayo. "Anything exciting?"

"Pre-law. I had grand plans of being a prosecutor someday, like my grandfather. But with all the crazy things going on in the world, I couldn't just sit by and do nothing, so I enlisted in the Army shortly after my first year. To my surprise, I found military life suited me better. I served for a few years before I was honorably discharged."

"Did that happen before or after you were changed?"

I stiffened as old memories surged, but I forced myself to relax. It might be good to talk about this with someone who could actually understand. "I was changed while on active duty in the Army."

"Wow." Celine placed her half-prepared bun on her plate, her appetite evidently forgotten. "That must have been tough to hide in the military."

I barked a laugh. "Luckily, I didn't have to worry about controlling my initial outbursts. During that time, I spent three weeks with a band of hybrid wolf-shifters in a Bolivian jungle."

"Yeah?" Celine blinked in surprise. "How did that happen?"

I sighed. "I was part of the Special Ops task force assigned to track someone down. We'd split up across the jungle to broaden the search, and my squad and I were attacked by a group of wolves. Apparently, we'd trespassed into their territory, not that there were any signs warning us away or anything."

"That's horrible." Celine's eyes were wide as she stared at me, her expression a combination of fascination and horror. "How on earth did you survive?"

"Another pack of wolves happened to be in the area, and they charged in, forcing the others to retreat," I recalled. "I learned later, the two packs were mortal enemies, always fighting for territory in the jungles. They were sympathetic to us since all of them had once lived in the nearby villages and towns before being forced into the jungles after being changed, so they took us in. They taught us the basics of how to control our inner beasts well enough to mingle among society, and then we made it back to our camp."

Celine frowned. "If they knew how to mingle with society, then why were they hiding out in the jungle instead of living among people?"

I shrugged. "Most of them had been abandoned by their families or just couldn't bring themselves to face the people they'd left behind. Some preferred the wild, deciding to live in a community of people they didn't have to hide from. I have to admit, I understand where they're coming from. It's tough to try to coexist with people who don't understand you."

Celine nodded. "I know how that is. I'm lucky I at least got to grow up with a family who was the same as me," she remarked, a faraway look in her eyes. She blinked and refocused on me. "So, what happened after that? Did you continue in the military?"

I shook my head. "My squad and I were honorably discharged after being diagnosed with post-traumatic stress disorder." I snorted. "I spent some time messing around. Then Jimmy, with whom I used to serve, offered me a job in New York. So, here I am."

Celine raised an eyebrow. "So, that's it? You go from being on a task force in the Army to doing security detail at an art museum with no bumps in between?"

"Yes. There were bumps...but let's leave it at that for now." I crossed my arms and changed the subject, not willing to discuss Julia with Celine just yet. "So, this place of yours...it's a beautiful spot," I praised, gesturing around the space. "How long have you lived here?"

"I like it a lot. Plus, I don't have any neighbors because the town house next door is empty. And, to answer your question, I've lived here a couple of years, but I actually spend most of my time at my dad's residence in New Jersey," she admitted ruefully. "My dad likes to keep me close, especially since my mother passed away. I bought this place a few years ago as a sanctuary with some of the money I'd made playing the stock market, and I come here whenever I need some space and peace and quiet."

I blinked. "So, you weren't lying about the stock market stuff?"

"Nope." Celine laughed and picked up her bun again, plopping the hamburger onto it along with some lettuce, tomatoes, and onions before closing it up. She took a huge bite and chewed for a few moments before speaking again, "My dad taught me about stocks when I was a young girl, and I always had a natural aptitude for it."

I raised a brow. "You'd think that, with a moneymaking skill like that, you wouldn't be so concerned about needing to inherit your father's empire."

Celine sighed. "I know what you're saying," she declared, toying with one of her curls, "but Dad is real old-school and wants to keep the business in the family, and I don't have the damn heart to deny him. He's always loved me and taken good care of me over the years. I figure the least I can do is make sure the business passes into the hands of someone who will keep it going. He's worked his entire life to build that business from the ground up. It's his legacy. I can't just watch it be destroyed without stepping in to save it."

I nodded. "Totally understandable. How did Carter get involved in the business?"

Celine trembled at the mention of his name, and I reached out to her from across the table, taking her hand into mine. She looked up at me, lips quivering, blinking back tears.

It was a few moments before she spoke, "When the economy took a nose dive, Dad needed to take on investors. Carter was the only one who really had the ability to save the company from going bankrupt. Dad managed to keep the majority share, but Carter wanted a large stake in the company. And Dad wasn't in a good situation to refuse him, so he took the fucked-up offer."

"Your dad had no idea what kind of man he was doing business with?" I replied, my voice soft and soothing.

"No. Dad would never have agreed if he knew. No one knew. When Carter came to me, asking me to be his mate, I refused, but then he told me of his intentions...the reason he'd saved my dad's company in the first place. He wanted me."

I gently stroked Celine's hand before moving my chair so I could be closer to her.

"I just didn't want Dad to lose everything else when he had already lost Mom," she confessed, choking back tears. "He's lost so much already. We both have. That's the only reason I made a vow to Carter, and according to shifter law, my promise can only be broken if a shifter challenges our union and wins the battle."

I wrapped my arm around her shoulder and nuzzled her against me for a moment. "It's going to be okay Celine."

Now I knew exactly what I had to do to free her from Carter, and if things were on stronger terms between us, I'd challenge Carter without hesitation.

WE FINISHED THE REST OF OUR MEAL IN comfortable silence and then worked together to clean up the kitchen.

"I guess I'd better head back home," I announced, shrugging my jacket back onto my shoulders. I hated to leave her here, but I knew that staying with her would only complicate things between us.

"Please, don't go." Celine grasped my

sleeve, her large eyes imploring as she looked up at me.

She bit her bottom lip. The gesture was so vulnerable and sexy at the same time that I nearly groaned in frustration.

"Gunner, I don't want to be alone tonight."

I couldn't really fault her for that, especially since I didn't really want to leave her alone either.

"Please stay," she whispered.

"All right," I answered quietly, while making a mental note to text Jimmy to ensure he wouldn't need his car. "I'll stay." I glanced at the couch. "So long as you have some extra blankets?"

Celine followed my gaze. "No," she blurted. "What I mean is, you don't have to sleep on the couch. There's a guest room upstairs. Or..."

"Or what?" I didn't miss the way her pulse had jumped in her throat or the longing in her eyes as she gazed up at me.

Don't give in.

"Nothing." She sighed heavily. "Let me show you to your room, so we can get some sleep."

I followed her up the stairs, staring at her sexy, voluptuous ass swaying mere inches from my face, and I wondered if I was going to be able to get any sleep at all tonight.

I concluded...most definitely not.

I JERKED awake to the sound of soft whimpering. Blinking in the darkness, it took me a few moments to remember I was in Celine's guest room, decorated in the same bold colors and geometric patterns as the living room. Sitting up, I cocked my head, realizing the sounds were coming from Celine's room across the hall.

She must be having a bad dream.

I hesitated, wondering if I should go check on her or give her some privacy. But the whimpers quickly escalated to sobs, and I bounded out of the bed and into the master bedroom across the hall before I really even had time to think about what I was doing.

"Shh," I whispered.

Celine was thrashing around in the sheets, so I sat down on the edge of the bed, turning on the lamp sitting on the bedside table, and lifted her into my arms.

"It's all right. You're safe."

"Please stop! No more!" she cried, simultaneously cringing and flailing as I settled her into my lap. "Why won't you stop?"

"Shh." I rocked her gently, pushing down the sudden surge of bloodlust at her words. I wanted to find Carter and rip him limb from limb. "He's not here, baby. He can't hurt you anymore." I continued to murmur reassurances until she eventually calmed down, growing limp in my arms, twisting around so that she could curl herself up against me.

Her eyes snapped open. "I'm sorry," she muttered into my bare chest.

I'd only worn my boxers to bed, and I hadn't thought to put on a shirt in my haste to get to her.

"That was stupid of me."

"It's not stupid," I murmured, stroking her hair as I continued to rock her. I paused for a moment before adding, "Sometimes, I still have nightmares, too."

"Really?" Celine looked up, her green eyes luminous in the moonlight that spilled in through the windows. "About your attack?"

I nodded. "Less than I used to, but yeah, they still happen every once in a while."

"I'm sorry." She buried her face into my chest again. "Please, Gunner...stay in here with me. I need you to keep the nightmares away."

Wordlessly, I acquiesced, rolling back onto the bed so that I spooned her from behind, and I pulled the sheet over us both. Closing my eyes, I tucked my head into the crook of her shoulder, burying my face in her hair, and tried to relax. But the scent of her shampoo mixed with her own unique, enticing scent teased my nostrils. The round curves of her ass pressed deliciously into my groin. Instantly, my pulse shot up with my heart pumping blood into my nether regions. I gritted my teeth, trying to resist the hard-on I knew was growing.

I heard Celine draw in a breath, and then I nearly cursed as I scented her own arousal. Holding myself rigidly still, I tried not to move, not to breathe, hoping like all hell that this would pass and we would both fall asleep. But she shifted in my arms, her ass rubbing against my erection, and I nearly groaned out loud.

She'd have to be dead to miss that.

I thought she would settle down after a moment, but instead, her ass kept brushing up against my cock, and I realized she was doing it on purpose.

"You little vixen," I growled, grabbing her around the waist, forcing her to hold still. Unfortunately, that caused her ass to press up tightly against my pulsating cock, and this time, I really did groan out loud. "Celine? Are you trying to kill me?"

"Sorry!" she exclaimed, not sounding the least bit regretful. "I think it's an involuntary reaction."

She rubbed her ass against me again, and I let out another groan.

"I can't seem to help it. My ass has a mind of its own."

"Shit. I knew this was going to happen," I moaned. My hands gripped the waistband of her yoga pants. I barely managed to stop myself from yanking them down around her knees and taking her right there.

Celine turned her head, facing me, hurt shimmering in her eyes. "Are you saying you don't want me?"

"Of course, I want you," I countered with an exasperated huff. "That's the whole problem. I'm not supposed to want you. You're supposed to..." I trailed off.

She's supposed to what, exactly? Be with Carter? There is no way in hell I am letting her marry that sick fuck. Not after what he did to her tonight. If I had to go track down her father and tell the guy myself, I would do it if it meant her safety.

"You're the only one I want, Gunner," Celine confided softly, completely turning around in my arms and now facing me. "We both know we're meant to be together, and I'm tired of trying to fight it."

She kissed me before I could respond, sliding her tongue into my mouth, and whatever I'd been about to say flew straight out of my damn head as my sensory perception burst into overdrive.

Crushing her to me, I devoured her mouth with single-minded purpose, wanting to drink her in until I was filled to the brim, though part of me knew I would never truly be satiated. Growling, I slid a hand beneath the waistband of her pants, squeezing her left cheek before moving between her legs to caress the soft, wet folds waiting for me.

"Yes," she moaned. She dug her fingers into my shoulders and tipped her head back, exposing the elegant column of her throat. "More."

"Yes." I slid two fingers into her from behind, slowly pushing in and out, while ducking my head so I could nibble on the sensitive flesh near her collarbone. I inhaled the scent of her sweet arousal, which was growing stronger by the second, until I felt as if I were drunk on it, my head swimming from the deliciously heady scent.

"Careful," I ordered, gently turning her over onto her stomach. "I don't want to hurt you." I pushed her pants down to her knees, positioning her so her ass was thrust up higher in the air than her shoulders. But instead of sliding into her, I spread her knees wider and started licking her pussy.

"Oh!" Celine jerked in surprise, quickly followed by a moan as I sucked her clit. "Yes, please, please, please don't stop..." She trailed off into incoherent cries as I finger-fucked her again, consumed by the need to push her over the edge.

My inner beast howled triumphantly as she came hard and fast, shuddering against my mouth and fingers.

"And you can't hurt me. You could never hurt me."

"I can't wait any longer," I growled, my voice rough as I rose up onto my knees and yanked off my boxers. "I need to be inside you now."

"Condom," she whispered. "I think there's one in the bedside table…"

Quickly, I reached over, opening the table and finding a gold condom packet. Tearing open the wrapper, I sheathed my cock. Gripping her hips, I filled her with a single thrust, nearly groaning aloud as her tight core squeezed my cock. As I began moving inside her, she pushed her hips back up against mine, meeting me thrust for thrust, and I couldn't help but think she was the sexiest woman I'd ever seen as she looked over her shoulder at me. Her hair falling around her face and spilling across her back, she gave me a smoking-hot, wanton stare, scorching me all the way to my toes.

"Harder," she demanded, pushing more firmly against me. "Faster."

"But I don't want to hurt you," I hissed.

"You won't. I'm already fully healed. Shifter, remember? Now, please, harder," she begged me.

I complied with her request, slamming into her with a hunger and ferocity I knew might hurt a human woman but only seemed to excite Celine. Her moans grew louder and louder until she finally came again, her pussy clenching tightly around my cock as she shuddered. White light exploded in my vision as her release triggered my own, and I gripped her against me as my hot seed spilled inside the condom. Waiting a bit while she curled onto the bed tiredly, I went to the bathroom to dispose of the condom. Wasting no time, I came back to her.

I love you, I wanted to murmur aloud as I drew her back against me, lying down on our sides and tucking her into my body as she drifted off into what I hoped would be a peaceful, dreamless sleep. *I fucking love you, woman.* But I couldn't say it, not until I was really sure she was ready to hear it.

Soon, she'll be mine, I vowed before nodding off to sleep. *I'll find a way to fix this, and then we can be together...forever.*

16

CELINE

I WOKE up to the sound of someone pounding on my front door. Groggily, I sat up and pushed my hair out of my face, dread pooling in my stomach as I wondered who the hell it could be. It was still dark out, so I hadn't been asleep for long.

"Open the door!" Carter yelled, pounding on the door again. "I'm not done with you, Celine!"

Shit. With all the racket he was making, I thanked God I didn't have neighbors to witness his embarrassing display.

"That twisted bastard," Gunner seethed, already on his feet. "Stay here."

"Wait..." I started to say, but Gunner was

already out the door and storming into the guest room.

Quickly, I hopped out of bed, running over to my dresser, yanking it open and pulling out a tank and sweats. I tugged them on with fear pulsing through my veins as I wondered why the fuck Carter was here. It didn't take Gunner long to come out of the guest room, tugging on his jeans.

"I'll handle this shit," he barked.

"Shit. Gunner, no." Rushing down the hall and stairs, I made it just in time to see Gunner fling open the door to confront Carter.

"What the hell do you want?" Gunner barked.

"You!" Carter roared, his eyes flashing gold. "You've tarnished her...ruined her with your filthy hybrid scent. I've waited a long time for her, and you're not going to stop me. She's mine! Now, get the fuck out of my way!" He pushed Gunner with enough force to make him stumble back a bit, giving him enough space to enter the house.

I trembled with rage as Carter's red-hot gaze focused on mine.

"Celine, stand back." Gunner stepped between us, shielding me with his huge, muscular body. "Carter, if you take another step toward her, I'll fucking kill you."

Carter bared his teeth, showing his elongating canines. "You can try, hybrid, but I'm stronger than I look," he sneered. "A hybrid against a pure-blooded shifter? You don't stand a damn chance."

"Not another step." Gunner planted his feet, clearly readying himself for an attack. "I'm warning you."

"Why are you even here, hybrid? It's not like Celine would ever be permitted to mate with the likes of you. So, what exactly do you want?"

"I want you to let her the hell go. Sell off your shares in her father's company and leave her and her family the fuck alone."

"Oh, you can't be damn serious," Carter snarled. "I won't allow you to take what is rightfully mine. Move aside."

"She's not yours," Gunner growled, refusing to budge. "She'll never be yours, Carter."

"Is that so?" Carter snarled. "And why is that? Because a hybrid like you is going to stop me from claiming her?"

"Yes, that's right." Gunner bared his own teeth, and I saw a ripple shiver across his body as his teeth lengthened, fur bursting from hidden hair follicles.

On Gunner's skin, a thicker coat of fur continued to sprout from his forearms. He looked lethal as razor-sharp claws pushed through his flesh until fingers became monstrous paws as he let his animal out. His beast wasn't in full form like a pure-blooded shifter, but he looked stronger than he did in his human form. As a hybrid, he would never be a full wolf, only half man, half beast, but he was far more powerful in this form.

"I've done my research on the governing laws of your pack, fucker!" Gunner shouted. "And according to shifter law, as Celine's true mate, I have the right to challenge you. Unless you'd just prefer to surrender?"

"Surrender? Not a chance, hybrid!" Carter's eyes were full gold now, his face bright red with anger. His eyes shifted toward me. "Is this true? Is he really your mate?"

I nodded. "He is."

He stared at me for a long moment, frozen in disbelief. "Well, I don't care," he jeered, shaking his head while ripping off his jacket and tossing it aside. "I won't let you take what's mine. I accept your challenge."

Without further warning, he lunged at Gunner. The two of them met in a clash of muscles, claws, and fangs. Gouging long scrapes and cuts into each other's skin and pounding fists into each other's faces and bodies, struggling for the upper hand. It was almost too fast to follow, but my enhanced vision allowed me to keep up. I winced as Carter slammed Gunner into the wall, causing a spider web of cracks to spread out across the spot on the wall and a potted plant to fall off a nearby table. With the amount of noise they were making, I was grateful I didn't have neighbors, or the police would have been here already.

"Gunner!" I screamed, wanting to rush in and pull them apart even though I knew I couldn't.

Once a challenge was issued, no one was allowed to interfere.

I had to let this play out, no matter what happened.

I shuddered, wrapping my arms around myself in an attempt to calm my wildly beating heart. I had given my word to Carter years ago, and as a shifter, that word was binding, broken only if another challenged the union and won. However, if Carter won, I would be forced to be his mate.

You have to win, Gunner. You just have to.

Gunner pushed Carter back to the middle of the room, and the two were exchanging blows again.

Suddenly, Gunner moved in, managing to hook a leg around Carter's foot, pulling him into a takedown. The two men landed hard, Carter taking most of the impact. Gunner took advantage of the moment, pummeling him with nonstop blows to the face and body. Carter snarled and writhed beneath him, trying to find purchase so he could get the upper hand. Gunner was relentless though, beating him down until he finally got Carter into a choke hold. Elation filled me at the sight.

He was going to win.

"Surrender," Gunner demanded, his own eyes glowing gold. "Surrender, or I'll kill you."

"You won't kill me," Carter hissed with what little breath he had. "You don't have the guts, hybrid," he practically spat the words.

Gunner cursed loudly, though he didn't let go of Carter. He hesitated, as if he didn't want to kill Carter. "Just give up, Carter."

"Never," Carter snarled. "I will never let her go. I paid for that bitch many times over, and she's mine!"

Gunner let out a shattering growl, singing loudly of his rage. Without hesitation, he swiped at Carter, his claws gleaming in the moonlight. He made contact with Carter's neck, and blood spurted into the open air, spraying the walls and floors.

Carter howled, his beast quickly taking over. Golden fur sprouted over his body, his face expanded until a snout appeared, his yellowing canines half descended.

Carter crouched, his hindquarters tensing, as he prepared to lunge. He jumped into the air, landing on Gunner and pinning him down. His jaw snapped, and he bit down into Gunner's shoulder. Gunner howled in pain, blood instantly seeping through his fur, staining the thick coat of hair in a pool of dark red. Carter roared, as if reveling in the taste of his opponent's blood.

Gunner fought for dominance, a blur of gnashes with low growls rippling from his throat. He leapt at Carter, and Carter fell to the floor with a hard thud. Gunner immediately dived for Carter's soft underside, his teeth tearing at the thick fur.

Carter was a powerful opponent, and he fought hard against Gunner, refusing to surrender. He twisted, kicking at him with his back legs. Gunner momentarily lost his grip and sprang back as Carter leaped to his feet. Carter bellowed with a growl that shook the house, threatening to break the glass windows. A growl that screamed, this wouldn't be over until only one of them was left breathing.

Gunner glanced over at me and lost all focus as he took me in. In my angst, I had shifted into my wolf. I stood with a coat of raven fur. I was terrified for Gunner, and then something happened that I'd never experienced before.

I heard his voice in my head.

He spoke to me telepathically, *You're my true mate. I will never let him hurt you again.*

With a snarl, he stood with his feet spread wide, his posture strong. The stance of a champion. His teeth were bared, and he carefully watched Carter, who was unhurriedly circling in what had now become a fight to the death. Carter slowly advanced, but in a flash of fur and yellow teeth, he jumped into action, and Gunner watched as he bounded at him with full force.

Gunner crouched low, swiping Carter's front legs with fingers tipped with razor-sharp claws. He caught Carter off guard, and the beast staggered, tumbling to the ground. Gunner seized the opportunity to gain the upper hand and tackled Carter, his claws digging into his flesh, resulting in gaping wounds. Gunner didn't let up, his long, sharp claws easily cutting through Carter's coat, leaving jagged lines behind.

He dug his claws into Carter's neck, and fresh blood spurted from the torn jugular vein. The beast made a horrible gurgling noise, twisting feebly beneath him. Waves of blood ran over the floor, leaving everything it touched with a scarlet sheen.

It was over, more quickly than I'd thought possible. Gunner sat back, looking down at the ruined creature beneath him. Its matted fur was wet with blood. Its chest drew one last shallow breath and then stilled.

Shifting back into my human form, I flew

into my mate's arms, clutching him. "Gunner! Oh, thank God!"

"He'll never hurt you again," Gunner growled through bared teeth, his body slowly returning to full human form.

A blessed silence fell over the room for a few seconds, and Gunner sighed in relief, refusing to let me out of his arms.

"I'm so glad you're okay," I sobbed as I clung to him. "I was so afraid."

"Shh. It's all right, darling. It's over now. You're free." He stroked my hair for a few moments, hugging me tighter. "I love you, Celine. I've loved you from the very first time I laid eyes on you, and I'll never stop."

"And I love you." Tears flowed down my cheeks as I stared at my unexpected hero. My mate and the man with whom I wanted to spend the rest of my life.

17

GUNNER

I SIGHED in relief as the door closed behind me, and I sank onto the king-size bed in the hotel we had temporarily moved in to at the insistence of Celine's dad, who finally knew the truth about Carter and all that I'd done to help his daughter.

Right after my brutal battle with Carter had finished, Celine had immediately called her dad, and he'd rushed over. It hadn't taken long for us to explain what had happened, and her father had called in a couple of favors to remove Carter's body. It wasn't the way I'd ideally imagined meeting her dad for the first time, but despite the unusual circumstances and the fact that I was a hybrid, her father had accepted me as the man his daughter wanted as her mate.

"What a week it's been," I groaned. "I think I need a drink."

"I think you need something, all right," Celine teased, laughing huskily as she plopped herself onto my lap.

I groaned again, but it was a halfhearted sound. "Oh, I'll always need this," I drawled before capturing her mouth for a kiss.

"Yes, and I need you," she replied, peeling off her shirt so I could caress her breasts. A moan escaped her lips as I took them into my palms, kneading them. "That is, if you think you can handle it," she finished with a coy look.

"Always."

Grinning, I kissed the tops of her breasts, my tongue sliding over her soft skin. Moaning, she allowed her head to fall back, her curls cascading wildly around her shoulders as she ground against me. She looked like a Valkyrie, and I was ready to ride with her straight into Valhalla.

I watched her just a moment longer. I pulled her toward me again, and my mouth descended on hers, devouring her in a kiss that took her breath away. My tongue skated along her plump lower lip, teasing and playing with her. She opened her mouth to me, her tongue dancing with mine.

Easing back, I tugged her to her feet with hands at the waist of her jeans, working the snap and zipper. I slid my fingers against her skin, cupping her voluptuous ass before caressing her curves.

"Take it off," I demanded.

Celine slid the jeans down her body, kicking them away, and then she took off her top.

"My turn!" she exclaimed before tugging me to my feet.

Her hands worked the front of my jeans, the bulge of my erection making things a bit difficult for her to unzip me. Finally, she had enough room to slide her fingers beneath the fabric to find my cock hot, hard, and ready. She stroked me slowly. I couldn't take the torture anymore and swooped down to kiss her, moaning against her mouth as I flexed my hips forward, forcing myself against her hand.

"God, I want you, Celine." My voice was

husky. I broke away from our kiss, and I looked down at her hand on my cock.

"Patience, mate," she ordered softly as she pulled me free of my jeans.

Her fingers wrapped around my shaft, caressing me, and it was sweet agony. I abruptly pulled away from her, picking her up and placing her onto the bed. Tugging off my jeans and shirt, I turned her over onto her stomach. She rose up onto her hands and knees then spread her legs. I got onto the bed, my legs spread, holding her legs apart with my knees.

I quickly took her, the weight of my body giving me momentum. My thrusts were hard and fast. She cried out as I grabbed a handful of her hair, tugging her head back. Celine spread her arms, and her hands curled into fists, grabbing the sheets.

Each push brought me closer, drove me farther into her warmth and wetness. I gritted my teeth, holding myself back, waiting for some kind of sign from Celine that she was close. I didn't want to deprive her, and I sensed she needed this, needed the force of my strokes to drive all conscious thoughts from her.

"You like this?" I asked, reaching around with one hand to stroke her clit.

"Yes," she moaned, pushing against my hand. "More."

Her muscles tightened around my cock, and I groaned, my pleasure intensifying.

It all seemed so easy, so effortless. She was held securely, lovingly, feeling every stroke I made, right to her core. There was nothing she needed to do but relax and let me take her on this ride.

It turned from a gentle, unhurried ride into something more, something wild and fierce and primal. I plowed into her, my breath rasping as I nuzzled her neck. Her fingers clutched the bedsheets, her nails digging into the silk material, holding on for dear life.

Then, everything was driven from my mind as my body took over, the heat building inside me, and I was consumed with satisfying my mate. I bit her shoulder, causing her to cry out, while she thrashed beneath me. I held her tight, containing the raging fire that threatened to destroy me.

When she came, it was hard and swift, her body convulsing and her hips jerking forward, pulling me down with her. I braced my knees on the bed, still moving, as she cried out beneath me. The contractions of her body around my cock grew stronger, and every cell in my body screamed for release. My breath tore from my throat. The fire in my lungs matched the heat in my balls and flooded up the shaft of my cock. It was inevitable, unrelenting and utterly beyond my control.

"You feel so good...too good," I panted, gripping her hips as I pumped even quicker.

My climax was so close, I could almost taste it. There was no holding back for me. Everything spun out of my control, and I plowed into a gasping Celine with short, sharp jabs as my body took over, my hips finding an erratic rhythm of their own. Her cries faded as my growls increased, and I tipped my head back, shouting in ecstasy.

Celine cried out, another orgasm cresting over her as she arched beneath me, and I spilled my seed inside her on a long, low moan. When there was no more left in me, I collapsed on top of her. My sweat-slicked chest pressed against her back, my cock sliding out of her. I pressed myself against the soft, giving flesh of her ass. My hips still flexed forward, my body not yet ready to relax.

Gradually, I pulled away from her, relaxing slowly. As Celine's legs were released, she stretched first one and then the other leg. She would have slid from the bed if I hadn't had one arm still wrapped around her waist.

I felt an inner peace, something I had never experienced in all my years. When I was with Celine, nothing else mattered. The earth stopped spinning. The intensity between us was so incredibly powerful, it took my breath away.

We lay in the warm darkness for a long time, bodies recovering, breathing and heartbeats slowing. Finally, Celine rolled over, fitting her body next to mine. She rose up as I slid one arm beneath her, and she rested her head on my shoulder.

Celine ran her hand over my chest, idly drawing circles on my skin. "What's next?"

My eyes searched hers for a moment. In one powerful movement, I rolled Celine onto her back, pinning her to the bed.

"You marry me." It wasn't a question. I

smiled and leaned forward, kissing her. "We have a houseful of children who look just like you. And I spend my life making you happy."

"Sounds like a wonderful plan to me," she replied, "alpha mine."

~

IF YOU LOVED GUNNER, YOU'RE going to devour Book #2, Eli. Keep reading for a sneak peek at **ELI!**

GET A FREE SEDONA VENEZ BOOK!

https://sedonavenez.com/free-book

SNEAK PEEK AT ELI
ELI / CHAPTER 1

I looked out the window of my apartment, brooding as I gazed at the woman passing through the courtyard three stories down. The moonlight gleamed softly against the silky tresses of her auburn hair, illuminating the skin of her forehead and hands. Her head was bent down as she adjusted the textbooks she carried in one arm, so I couldn't get a good look at her face, but that didn't matter. I'd know Olivia Giordano anywhere— whether she was dressed in a pink T-shirt and jeans, as she was now, or wearing nothing but mud and grass and her father's silk bathrobe, as she had once long ago when we were in love and high school sweethearts.

I smiled faintly at the memory. Those days had been good, even the rough ones, because Olivia was always around to brighten my life. Her father had been furious with her that day for ruining his favorite bathrobe. But Olivia had never sought to be anything other than what she was. That was why everyone loved her, had been drawn to her, like butterflies to a pool of nectar.

Just as I was then. Just as I am now.

I watched as she climbed the stairs, briefly disappearing and then emerging on the third-floor walkway on the other side of the courtyard. I wondered how she would react if she knew that I was standing here, observing her. That I'd tracked her down and moved in to the apartment across the complex from hers when I returned to Chicago three months ago. That I'd kept tabs on her ever since.

Would she welcome me with open arms and ask me where I'd been? Or would she be angry at my intrusion?

Sighing, I tried to step away from the window, but I couldn't. I knew Olivia was an obsession I needed to let go of, but my eyes remained glued to the window as she stopped in front of her apartment door and fished for her keys in her coat pocket. I admired the way her tight jeans accentuated her curves. Curves that had become more defined since I last saw her a few years ago. She'd grown from a spring bud into a summer blossom, and more than once, I'd wished I could take her in my arms and see just how much she'd grown up.

But that's impossible. I can't go back to Olivia. I can't even let her know I am back in town. If I did, I would get sucked back into the mob life again, and that's something I swore I'd never let happen.

Loving a mobster's daughter came with a high price. And Olivia and I had decided years ago that it wasn't worth paying. So, now, I had to be content with only looking after her, even if it was from a distance.

She closed the door behind her, and I turned away from the window and wandered over to the kitchen to grab a beer from the fridge. Normally, I'd be at the shifter club on Rush Street, working as a bouncer, but I'd been given the night off. I loathed the long nights off. I never seemed to know what the hell to do with myself. I liked being at the bar. It gave me comfort to be with others of my kind. A sort of camaraderie I never felt anywhere else—at least, not since I'd returned from war.

It was funny how I felt like such an outcast in the city where I'd grown up. The city I'd thought I'd known like the back of my hand. Now, a few years later, I wondered if I'd really known anything at all.

Slipping my hand into my pocket, I drew out the gold pocket watch Dad had given me before he died many years ago. It was the most valuable thing he had ever owned, a Civil War relic, and consequently, it was now the most valuable thing I owned. Though Dad and I'd had our ups and downs, I'd held on to it all these years, and it gave me solace every time I pulled it out to look at it.

I was taking a swig from my beer when my cell rang, nearly startling me into dropping the bottle. Scowling, I glanced at the screen, not recognizing the number and wondering who the hell was calling me at this time of night. The only phone calls I ever got were from the club when they needed me to come in early. And now that I was home and comfortable, I suddenly found I didn't necessarily want to haul my ass down to Rush Street when the nightlife was already in full swing.

Swiping my finger across my cell, I answered, "McCauley."

"Eli!" a panicky, familiar voice burst through the line, accompanied by a faint crackling sound. "I'm so glad I reached you. Hey, how have you been, buddy?"

"Ian?" My blood ran cold at the sound of my old friend's voice.

Ian and I used to run with the mob back in the day—before I'd decided to call the gangster life quits and joined the military.

"How the hell did you get my number?"

I'd been deliberately avoiding all of my old friends, especially Ian, who had made a pact with me to quit the thug life and go straight. Then he'd backed out, only to return to the insanity. I didn't have any patience for those who tried to drag me down. Not after all I'd been through and how hard I had worked to clean up my life and go straight.

"Silvia gave it to me."

Shit.

Silvia was a former friend of Dad's, whom I'd run into weeks ago by accident. She also happened to be Ian's estranged aunt. Now, I was kicking myself for giving her my number, but I'd felt bad for her when she told me that her husband just died and she was all on her own with no one to help her with small errands.

"Look, Eli, I know I'm the last person you want to hear from right now," Ian said. "But I... Eli, I need your help."

I gave an exasperated sigh. "What are you in for this time, Ian? Racketeering? Extortion?"

"No, I'm not—"

"Sorry, Ian, but I can't help you. I don't have any money to front you for bail. Not this time. If you didn't want to end up in the tank, you should have gone straight, like I did. You've had so damn many opportunities to get out of that mess."

"I'm not in jail!" Ian burst out. "And I haven't been running any rackets or dealing or anything like that in a long time. I have been an honest guy for the past few years,

Eli. Really. It's just that I've never been able to shake the gambling, you know, and—"

"Hello, Eli." A different voice came on the line, one with an Italian accent that sent a trickle of sweat down my spine. "It's Nick Santorini. I used to know your father very well. I'm sure you've heard of me."

"Hi, Nick," I replied carefully. My mind was racing as I tried to figure out what the hell this guy wanted with me.

Nick Santorini was a capo for the Chicago Outfit, the Italian mobster organization my dad used to belong to. I had worked for them indirectly via the street gang I used to run with. I'd quit the business shortly after Dad was shot during a gang fight, but I remembered Nick as one of Dad's drinking buddies.

"Sure. What can I do for an old friend of my father's?"

"Ah, so you do remember! That's good," Nick replied with a chuckle. "See, I wasn't sure if you would, what with you being gone so long. I'm really sorry to interrupt your conversation with your buddy Ian over here, but I felt like he wasn't adequately explaining the situation to you, and I just wanted to help him out."

"Sure," I replied, feeling a cold lump of lead drop into my stomach. I could already see where this was going, and I cursed myself for being stupid enough to answer the call. "What exactly is the situation?"

"Well, see, Ian's gotten himself into a bind here," Nick explained. "He's got a fairly good eye for poker, but he slips up when he's drunk, and he owes one of our casinos quite a chunk of money."

I bit back a groan. "How much?"

"Well, it's in the six figures. Ian's a good kid though, and we've been trying to work with him on the payments, but I'm afraid the boss has run out of patience. Either he's got to pay up now, or we're going to have to pull the deal, if you know what I'm saying."

I swallowed, knowing what that meant. They were going to kill Ian if he didn't quickly pay the debt. There was no way my old friend was going to be able to come up with anything close to the amount that would assuage the Outfit once they got blood in their eyes.

"I'm not sure what I can do to help, Nick. I don't have six figures to lend Ian."

"Well, I figured you wouldn't, with you just coming back from the military and all." Nick chuckled.

"How did you know that?" I snapped.

Shit. Shit. Shit.

"Ian told me. Anyway, I wish soldiers got paid that kind of cash, but that just isn't how it goes. Nah, I'm not after you to try to squeeze you for cash, sonny. What I want is your expertise."

"My expertise?"

"Yeah, that's right. See, good soldiers are getting tougher to find these days, especially with the FBI cracking down on us harder than they used to. The boss is starting up a new business opportunity, and we can't have guys on board who are going to turn into informants and go running off to witness protection. Bad for business." He paused for a moment and then continued, "I remember you did good work back in the day, sonny, and I want you to come and work for us again. If you do, we'll consider Ian's debt paid in full."

"I see," I replied slowly.

I wholeheartedly wished I could reach through my cell and throttle the shit out of Ian. Doing so would certainly save me a lot of damn trouble. But, deep down inside, I knew I couldn't let the mob kill Ian, not if there was a way for me to stop it. Though Ian was a weak-willed man, he'd always been there for me in the past and even saved my ass on a few occasions. I wouldn't be able to forgive myself if I turned my back on my old friend now.

"How long will I have to serve?" I countered.

"Excuse me?"

"How long will I have to serve the Outfit?" I rephrased my question. "If I'm doing this to pay off a debt, I'm assuming I won't be getting paid. I want to know how long I have to serve and whether or not I'm going to need to quit my job at the club and find a different one that'll fit better with my schedule."

"Oh, don't worry about keeping a second job. You'll still get paid," Nick assured me. "Maybe not as much as your father did, not with you starting off as a soldier and all, but you'll make enough to keep that nice little apartment you've got there. As for the time frame, I think five years is a good number to pay off $250,000, don't you, Ian?" I didn't hear Ian say anything in the background, but I assumed Ian nodded because Nick said, "Exactly. Five years, Eli. That's all we're asking for. Then you're free to get on with your life."

"Okay," I agreed, even though I knew Nick was lying.

Once you joined the mob, you were usually in for life unless you went to the Feds, offering to cough up valuable information in exchange for protection. Witness protection was the last place I wanted to go. Since I couldn't go back to the military again, I could see no alternative aside from letting the mob kill Ian. And even that wouldn't help now that they knew I was back in town and where I lived. They'd simply find some other way to leverage me back into the mob, and if that didn't work, they'd just kill me.

What the mob wants, the damn mob gets.

"That's what I wanted to hear!" Nick chuckled. "The boys will be so glad to hear you're back, Eli. They really will. We'll have something for you tomorrow, so be here by eight o'clock." He rattled off an address to me. "Ian will be here too, so you'll have a friendly face to look forward to."

"See you then, Nick."

I ended the call, knowing that my last few hours of freedom would soon be over.

~

Devour Book #2, **ELI!**

WANT FREE SEDONA VENEZ BOOKS?

Sign up for Sedona Venez's Newsletter and receive FREE BOOKS. In addition to the free stories, you will also get special pricing, exclusive previews and news of new releases.

GET A FREE SEDONA VENEZ BOOK!

Join Sedona's mailing list to be the first to know of new releases, free books, special prices and other author giveaways.

https://sedonavenez.com/free-book

ABOUT THE AUTHOR

USA TODAY BESTSELLING AUTHOR SEDONA VENEZ lives in New York City with her hot ex-military hubby—hooah—and their fur babies. She loves writing sizzling, sexy intricate stories about strong but broken characters who push limits, overcome their fears and risk it all for love.

Sedona loves to connect with readers!
www.sedonavenez.com